D1709469

Legends of the House of the Cretan Woman

Legends of the House of the Cretan Woman

as told by

Sheikh Sulaiman al-Kretli

and put into English by

R. G. 'John' Gayer-Anderson Pasha

illustrated by

Abd al-Aziz Abdu of Cairo

with a foreword by

Theo Gayer-Anderson

and a new essay on the House of the Cretan Woman by

Nicholas Warner

Arabic calligraphy by

Ahmed Sultan Gabriel

The American University in Cairo Press
Cairo · New York

The author
dedicates this book
to the Egyptian people

Contents

Foreword

by Theo Gayer-Anderson

"Fateful attractions"—the title of my grandfather's memoirs—is perhaps how the retired Major Robert Grenville ('John') Gayer-Anderson Pasha would have described how he came to spend so much of his life in Egypt. Initially it was the desire to travel and see the world, and the restless nature of a young man impatient for adventure, that spirited R.G. overseas. Barely twenty, having completed medical school at the earliest possible age, a promising international rugby player, a pioneer in the development of setting fractured limbs using external pins, with a practice already secured in Harley Street, he declared his intention of joining the army: a decision which must have perplexed his parents.

His first posting, as medical officer, was in Gibraltar, and as he embarked the troop ship he waved goodbye to his doting mother, his incredulous father, and a heartbroken Katharine (his one and only true love). By far the most painful separation, though, must have been from his twin brother Thomas, who had conspired with him in joining the army and was himself bound for India. From Gibraltar, R.G. was seconded to the Egyptian Army following a severe reprimand for a foolhardy and strictly prohibited foray across the sea to Tangiers, which was 'off limits' due to 'local upheavals.'

And so to Cairo, the Shepheard's Hotel, his dragoman dressed in silk, and his first encounter with the Bait al-Kretliya—the House of the Cretan Woman—where he was eventually to spend the happiest years of his life—but that story I will leave to my grandfather in his original introduction to this book. So what of the collector, the conservator, the poet, the regular contributor to the *Sphinx* and the *Egyptian Gazette*, the reclusive and slightly eccentric Major living in the comparative obscurity of the 'local quarters' of Cairo? My grandfather was a methodical man, and as he lay convalescing towards the end of his life in Little Hall, his Suffolk home, in the capable hands and good company of his brother, he must have dwelt on this paradox, and was perhaps in search of a solution as he began to write his memoirs.

RG Gayer-Anderson in Egypt, 1906

He attributed the turning point in his life to a single event, one that echoes an incident that occurred during the daring exploits in deepest Africa of John Gayer, a founding father of the Gayer-Anderson family, a merchant and explorer in the seventeenth century: John Gayer was saved from the jaws of a marauding lion, prowling outside his tent, by earnest prayers to God—and to this day his deliverance is celebrated annually with a service in London. R.G. Gayer-Anderson was plucked from the Sudanese wilderness five days after being separated from his hunting party. He was found naked, incoherent, and disheveled. After coming to in the officers' mess in Khartoum he picked up a mirror and found himself staring at a hollow-eyed and bearded stranger.

Rather than leave an endowment to a church for God's miraculous intervention, as his predecessor had done, he directed his energy away from the army into the more sedate and contemplative, but perhaps more rewarding, pastime of collecting antiques. On his return to Cairo, R.G. sold his polo ponies and bought books: he distanced himself from the social activities of a gentleman and an officer and, as he discreetly rose to the rank of Oriental Secretary under Lord Allenby, he acquired what might be described as a large and eclectic collection of small things.

R.G. eventually dispersed the bulk of the collection that he amassed in Cairo to the four corners of the Empire. Anyone who has visited either of his houses in Lavenham and Cairo, or has seen his bequests in museums from Canada to Australia, cannot but be touched by the endearing sensibility that resonates from every artifact he retrieved from oblivion. It is this very trait—the recognition of the inherent 'voice' of an object, of that which makes it unique and beautiful, of its intrinsic rather than monetary value—that makes his collections so accessible, and it is probably this that was meant when he was recognized as having a 'good eye.'

With this in mind, it is clear why my grandfather was so enamored with the stories he collected for this book, and why indeed he thought it worthwhile to share them with the world by publishing them. There are fourteen stories told, each effortlessly combining the magical and the everyday, the mysterious and the mundane, while weaving a fluid path through time encompassing pharaonic, Christian, and Islamic events. All take place within the walls of the Bait al-Kretliya or on the hallowed ground on which it stands. One might be under the impression, by the end of this book, that everything happened here.

The intentions of the storyteller himself, a previous occupier of the house, are also clear. He was ensuring that the new occupier took good care of the house, instilling *gravitas* into his mission by drawing on a wealth of ancient history and folkloric anecdotes. R.G. did indeed take care of the house, and when he sailed for England for the last time (circum-navigating Africa due to the Second World War, rather than passing Crete in the usual Mediterranean passage as he had done so many times before) he left behind a veritable jewel: one that all those who have beaten a path through the hustle and bustle of the narrow surrounding streets and reached the tranquility of its interior will attest to.

My grandfather is a hard act to follow, but it has long been my ambition, in the six years that I have lived and worked as a conservator in Cairo, to pay homage to him and his house in some way. Through the perseverance of Nicholas Warner, architect and historian, we have been able not only to reprint this book (originally published posthumously in 1951 by Thomas Gayer-Anderson) but have also initiated a project to help restore and enhance the house, the collections within, and its surroundings.

If you have visited the house, now the Gayer-Anderson Museum, already I am sure you will be pleasantly enchanted by the fourteen Legends of the House of the Cretan Woman, and if you are not acquainted with the museum I am equally certain that these stories will inspire you to venture forth. Fateful attractions indeed.

The author at home, 1924

Introduction

by the author

*If thou chance for to find
An house built to thy mind,
Without thy cost,
Serve thou the more
God and the poor;
And then my labour's not lost.*

By George Herbert from the
Chapter House of Southwell Cathedral

In the year 1906, as a young British Army doctor already enamoured of the East, I came to Cairo to join the Egyptian Army. Soon after my arrival, I set out one day from Shepheard's Hotel with a dragoman to see the sights, and one of the first places we visited was the great ninth century mosque of Ahmad Ibn Tulun, which stands in a very sacred but slummy part of Cairo. As I approached the Mosque I was lost in admiration of a fine stone-built house, a veritable castle, that rose before me and bridged over the passage to the main door of Ibn Tulun. Suddenly my attention was diverted by a pretty unveiled Egyptian girl who leaned out of one of the latticed windows of the first floor and called to me, smiling and beckoning.

"What does she say?" I enquired of my guide for I then had no word of Arabic.

"The shameless one invites you to view the old house."

"Is that all?"

"So it would seem."

"Shall we go in?"

"Be advised by me, Excellency, do not go in to her," answered my perhaps over-cautious companion, and I took his advice. I could not resist, however, advancing to the court of the house through the great entrance embellished with carved and coloured

5

The Bait al-Kretliya

stone-work and having a massive iron-studded wooden door that looked as though it had not been shut for hundreds of years. This court was surrounded by the high stone faces of the house with large windows of *mashrabiya* (an intricate lattice of turned wood typical of early Cairene houses) and a raised loggia on one side; the ground was strewn with refuse and litter of every description in the midst of which ragged children, moulting hens, a cat or two, and a fat-tailed ram besported themselves apparently on a footing of complete equality.

I gazed for long at this squalid and picturesque scene, so entranced by it that it made an indelible impression upon my mind; then my guide roused me from my reverie and, somewhat regretfully, I moved on with him to view the famous shrine we had come to see.

I knew not at the time the name of the house for we did not ask it, but that was my first introduction to the House of the Cretan Woman—the Bait al-Kretliya! It was as though Fate had given me a little glimpse into the future, yet would not reveal to me that some twenty-nine years later I would be lord of that dream-castle, and that in it I was to spend my eight fullest and happiest years. Yet so it was to be. The trivial incident I have just recorded proved to be the prelude to what I consider the crowning event of my life: the granting, after that long period, of my most cherished desire.

I retired from all official duties in 1924 after a crowded career, every day of which had been spent in the service of Egypt, the land I had come to love above all others (not excepting my native country) and for whose people I had and have a very sincere affection: so it was in that land of my adoption that I decided to spend my remaining years.

As an ardent collector and Orientalist throughout my adult life, I had for long been trying to find an ancient Arab house in Cairo to furnish, embellish, and inhabit; a house away from the everyday Europeanised side of Cairo, for I wished to be largely apart from my own kind and in closer touch with the Egyptian people.

Twice I had established myself in attractive flats in native houses but each proved to be too small and lacking one or more of the absolute essentials. Then, almost by chance so it seemed, just such a house as I had been seeking "swam into my ken"—a Mameluke house, one of the most beautiful and interesting specimens of early domestic Arab architecture left in Cairo, the Bait al-Kretliya, the very same house I had seen on that day in 1906 when, knowing nothing of Arab domestic architecture, I first visited Ibn Tulun.[1] Soon I occupied it and became its lord!

This miracle had come about in the following manner. One day in 1935 (it was the 23rd of February to be exact) I suddenly decided, for no particular reason, to pay another visit to Ibn Tulun, a Mosque of which I was particularly fond but which I had not vis-ited for a year or more. I felt I had been neglecting an old friend; I felt him calling me, if you will. After my siesta, therefore, I chartered a horse-cab and drove there at the leisurely pace of those old-fashioned vehicles. On arrival, I found the surroundings of the Mosque amazingly changed and improved since I had last visited it by the clearance of many slum hovels; now the great stone house, which bridges the lane leading to the Mosque's main entrance, stood out clear and fine and recalled to my memory as it always did when I visited Ibn Tulun the day, twenty-nine years earlier, when that pretty Egyptian girl called to me from one of its windows inviting me to enter.

The house had obviously been restored and workmen were still busy about it. My interest was so thoroughly aroused that I found myself wondering what it was called: I asked the foreman who was at hand and for the first time I heard its name: "They call it the Bait al-Kretliya," he said. He also told me that the Government had acquired it some years back and that its complete structural restoration was just finished; that now it was in perfect repair and the workmen were giving it a final clear-up. What the Government were going to do with it the overseer did not know; it was now an "Arab monument."

Suddenly, I sensed that this house was going to be mine; with a strong feeling of excitement I entered it and, accompanied by the foreman, wandered entranced from room to room. It was dusk before I started to drive back to my flat through the golden dust-filled air. I had not visited my old friend Ibn Tulun after all. Indeed, I had forgotten him because my head was filled with exciting plans and possibilities.

The Sheikh

Next day, taking my head servant with me, I drove early to the Bait al-Kretliya and, again accompanied by the foreman, looked all over it, prying into every nook and cranny. After that thorough examination I realised that it met my requirements in every way and I was more sure than ever that this great house was meant for me.

I made another thorough inspection on the third day and then, in a state of breathless excitement, I wrote to the Government Department concerned, applying to be allowed to occupy the Bait al-Kretliya rent-free for the remainder of my life on condition that when I vacated the House, I was to hand it back to the Egyptian State completely furnished and equipped in every way with my large Islamic collections. I also started pulling all the strings I could to hasten a satisfactory decision. With surprisingly little delay my request was granted: the Bait al-Kretliya was mine!

On 16th October, 1935, my occupation began—I slept in the House for the first time. The Ministry of Works were still in process of installing main water, modern sanitation, and electricity. Next day I began my tasks of internal decoration, the placing of my Islamic possessions, and the restoration or replacement of fountains, pavements, ceilings, and much else where the originals had been damaged, removed, or destroyed. Those tasks went steadily on during the whole of my occupation and were only just finished when, in 1942, ill-health forced me to give up that beloved dwelling.

I had not long taken over the Bait al-Kretliya before I met the Sheikh Sulaiman al-Kretli, head of the family from which the house took its name, "the onlie begetter" of the following tales. He called to pay his respects, for he was the hereditary custodian of the tomb of Sidi (my Master) Haroon al-Huseini (a direct descendant of the Prophet) whose remains lie buried under the small white dome at the corner of the tiny front garden.

Dear old Sheikh Sulaiman! I can see him now, clad in his long white *kuftan* (gown) and black *redingote*, a dingy red tarboosh on his head without the conventional holy man's white or green turban round about it. He wore several silver and turquoise rings on the fingers of both hands, which were deeply tobacco-stained, for he smoked cigarettes continuously while he drank innumerable cups of black coffee or sipped cinnamon tea.

He was a Sheikh, a *fikki* (holy man), a dervish of times past, such as one will never meet again. A little, bent old man of eighty maybe, who leaned heavily upon his stick as he hobbled along. His wrinkled, russet-apple face was fringed with white whiskers and a far from orthodox, unkempt white beard gave him the appearance of a Chinese philosopher. His expression was shrewd and his smile at times decidedly cynical.

His mien was humble yet authoritative, as befitted his calling; his voice was refined and well modulated from much recitation of the Koran; his tone often bantering and never subservient unless custom demanded some exaggerated assumption of subservience. His eyes had been 'burnt out' as he termed it when, as a youth, he had been trapped in a burning house from which his Saint, Haroon, miraculouly rescued him.[2] They were half blind in consequence and showed but little light of expression, yet to judge by what he could at times see and remark upon, there must have been shafts that pierced their darkness.

I think we understood each other from the first, and we formed one of those pleasant, perhaps rather insincere, and therefore unexacting friendships. I was certainly impressed by him from the moment he tottered across my courtyard to introduce himself, loudly proclaiming "*Mashallah*" (as Allah wills) as he approached.[3] He was followed by a buxom wife still in her forties who often accompanied him, seating herself unobtrusively on a corner of the floor while her lord and I conversed, installed side by side on a divan in the lofty arched *maq'ad* (loggia) of the house.

I had already discovered that the older of my neighbours greatly venerated the House and its locality, and of course the Sheikh specially so, and small wonder, for he and his fathers before him during the past hundred years and more (not eight hundred years as he was wont to declare, for his ideas as to dates and periods were very sketchy) had been born in the tiny birth-room of the Bait al-Kretliya and brought up in that family house until, quite recently, it had been bought from him and his kin by the Government. Now nothing of the Family's original possession remained to him as its head, save the hereditary custodianship of the tomb of Sidi Haroon, beneath whose pearl-like dome he had passed the major part of his existence ever since his eighth year, immured in this cheerful whited sepulchre wherein beneath an imposing catafalque rest the bones he tended.

It was not long before I sensed that, surrounding and enmeshing Sidi Haroon and his tomb, the

9

House and its magic well, the Mosque, and the neighbourhood in general, there was a network of legends which the Sheikh had acquired during his long life—though he had never recorded them—and soon I began to question him concerning that complicated web.

At first he spoke with diffidence of "such foolish tales" as though fearing ridicule, but when he saw that I was seriously interested and actually produced pencil and paper and wrote down the words from his mouth, he gained confidence and warmed to an enthusiasm which never deserted him thereafter, though I was pressing in my demands.

The East still depends largely on the spoken word for its entertainment, and no part of it is richer in folk-yarns than Egypt, where the Cairo-born *Arabian Nights* first made its appearance. From early days I had loved listening to story-tellers, professional or amateur, reciting such ancient tales as after much telling had become half truths, and I had already become a practised tale-collector, so the technique was not new to me. It was only to be expected that this historic House of the Kretlis would have its own array of tales and legends waiting for me to set down from the lips of the Sheikh, its head. Naturally enough, he was at times inclined to repeat himself and to bring too much family history into his narration but this I did not attempt to check, though I only recorded such of it as I considered interesting and more or less relevant; the result is sometimes rather a mixture, though not an unpleasant one. In this narration, the Sheikh seemed to modify his everyday mode of speech and at times to cast aside his years and assume youthful poetic diction. As might be expected, a considerable proportion of the tales proved to be too trivial, crude, or repetitive to be worth recording, so I discarded them. The few I have now selected, however, constitute an integral part of the history of the old House and its immediate neighbourhood. The four that are derived from Koranic sources come first, as affording a background to the rest which, like most Eastern legends, are a mixture of very doubtful ancient 'history' embroidered with superstition and fancy.

It will be seen that the Legends, whether of the Mosque, of the House, or of the Well, centre round the tomb of the Saint, the focus of Sulaiman's life.

That life had become a very routine affair, though far from uninteresting or uneventful. Ever since his House had "fallen" and he had been obliged to lodge elsewhere, the old man would hobble across from his sleeping quarters each morning at sunrise, unlock the tomb door, slip off his shoes, and step over the threshold straight into sanctity (right foot first, of course) with the pious remark, "*Mashallah*"; next, with an ejaculation "*Ya Allah*" ("Oh God"), he would spread out his *firwa* (sheepskin rug) and, squatting upon it, would soon be lost in profound meditation. After a while, rousing himself, he would begin to heat on a small charcoal brazier the day's supply of coffee which he had brought with him in a copper receptacle; as the morning wore on the usual passers-by, or itinerant vendors, or anxious old women would make their way to the tomb of Haroon and, each with raised hand after a short whispered prayer to the Saint, would pass on again to the daily routine. Later, friends and clients would begin to appear, coming or going, chiefly women, for although the old man gave advice like a spiritual lawyer to all and sundry on both sacred and mundane matters, it was mostly to women that he appealed and so he specialized in their affairs. They would come one after the other and squat for long spells, whispering into his ear while he nodded like the father confessor he was. He would contrive, at a price, complex *hagabat* (Koranic charms) for the begetting of children, retaining a husband's affection, confuting rivals, or encouraging lovers and, above all, for averting the evil eye.

Besides being a counsellor and composer of charms, philtres, and talismans, Sheikh Sulaiman was also a sorcerer versed in magic and mysteries of all sorts, but especially in *mandal* (divination).[4]

At sunset, his day over, he would depart, reversing the ritual of his arrival, locking the tomb door, and wending his way home.

Despite the wealth of information the Sheikh gave me, and the fact that his only recompense from me was coffee or cinnamon tea and cigarettes, he seldom solicited favours for himself or his family; but concerning the welfare of his charge, Sidi Haroon, his demands were frequent, insistent, and quite unabashed.

One day, shaking his finger almost menacingly in my direction, he exclaimed in a truculent tone, "How is it, Oh Honoured One, that you see fit to dwell in a palace of light while our master Haroon must remain in darkness? Yesterday, while I was in meditation, the Saint came again to me, saying, 'In his great house the Bey has brilliant illuminations in each and all of his many rooms, while here in my single chamber, which is but another room to his house, there is no light save that which my presence suffuses and your few guttering candles give forth, wherewith to read from the Koran over my head'." Needless to say, I had a powerful electric light installed next day.

On another occasion, not long after my taking up residence in the Bait al-Kretliya, we were drinking our coffee in the *maq'ad* when he suddenly exclaimed in a reproving voice, grasping my hand persuasively, "*Ya azizi* ("Oh dear friend") our master came to me last night while I slept. In anger he came, saying, 'For years past, my *moolid* (saint's day) has not been celebrated, save in the humblest and most miserable fashion, owing to thy abject poverty; but now, with this well-disposed and opulent Englishman here in our midst, see to it that at the beginning of the month of Shaaban each year there shall be three days' festival held in my honour which all the poor may attend'." Forthwith I saw to it that the three days' festival was revived, and it has been observed ever since.

In like manner, a dozen additions and improvements—all of which I was only too glad to have suggested to me—were carried out in and around the Saint's tomb with his entire approval, as voiced through his custodian, who assured me that many blessings continued to be heaped upon my head as, indeed, in the health and happiness I enjoyed at this time, I feel they were.

It was not until I had lived in the Bait al-Kretliya for about a year that I learnt that at first there had been considerable feeling aroused amongst the local inhabitants by the fact that a house with such sacred and legendary Islamic associations should be in the occupation of a Christian European, and I believe this feeling was overcome chiefly by the good offices of the Sheikh (through his intercession with the Saint), for he missed no opportunity of impressing upon the local inhabitants (many of them very tough and rough characters) that I was their sincere friend, out to help them and their dependants, as indeed was the case. There is no doubt, also, that the various things I did for the tomb of the saint, and the restoration of his *moolid,* influenced local opinion in my favour. The fact remains that it was not long before I felt that I had the confidence—and even the affection—of my neighbours and this, I think, was proved by their numerous visits to me in quest of advice, help, and medical first-aid.

Sometimes Sheikh Sulaiman, in his blind, stumbling manner, would walk round the Bait al-Kretliya with me, explaining how things had been in his day, recalling old happenings, and telling in detail the uses of the various rooms, cupboards, and crannies: "Here were the medicines kept"—"There our wax candles were stored"—"At one time there was a small door here that let directly into the tomb of Sidi Haroon, and no door into the tomb from outside existed, but that was reversed by my father's father."

The Sheikh's father, when master of the house, had been a man of substance and leisure, wont to spend much of his time seated in the *maq'ad* with his friends over coffee and pipes while his young children scampered about and were petted and pampered by him and his guests.

Sheikh Sulaiman himself had spent much of his early childhood across the courtyard in the *hareem,* as do most young Egyptian boys, amidst the constant comings and goings of women; mothers, aunts, wives, slaves, lady visitors, and go-betweens. Here,

there was always an atmosphere of interest and excitement over bargaining for lengths of brocade, arranging betrothals, accouchements, and circumcisions, procuring Sudanese women to exorcise devils from those unhappily possessed, or else the multifarious traffickings in the courtyard below, where many daily household affairs were transacted, and the purveyors of food, water-carriers, and sherbet-sellers plied their trades.

Sometimes the courtyard would act as a stage, where the men from the *maq'ad* on the left, and the women from the windows of the *hareem* opposite it, could all watch the contortions of acrobats, the dancing girls, the performances of snake-charmers, shadow-shows, whirling dervishes, performing apes, and other itinerant entertainments that were always in request.

The house had its sombre memories too—old age, sickness, and death—tragedies of envy and malice—periods of plague and famine; but all these evils seem to have been mitigated for the Sheikh's family by the benign presence of Sidi Haroon, or by the kindly intervention of the "agatho demon," the family serpent about which one of the following legends relates.

As time went on, the fortunes of the Family fluctuated, as those of all families must, and finally they declined. The Kretlis fell on evil days; eventually the property became divided among many inheritors and mortgagees who broke it up into small tenements which they sublet or lived in themselves. "Now our beautiful *hareem* was transformed into a bakery, and the big *qa'ah* of the *salamlik* was made into two storeys by adding a floor and partitioned off into many small, squalid apartments." At last, little seems to have been left as it had been in the lovely original home, save the tomb chamber, and this the Sheikh continued to tend as though nothing were amiss. "I knew all the time," he declared to me, "that Sidi Haroon would not let the house be submerged in ruin."

The Sheikh was right, for at length, as I have said, the property was sold outright to the Government (the best thing that could possibly have happened to it) and from then its vicissitudes were at an end. Cleared from its shabby surroundings (as the Great Mosque had already been), its grace and beauty—which had been lost or submerged for so long—were restored to it. It was reborn.

Sheikh Sulaiman looked on with those dull, seeing eyes of his faith at this miracle, vouchsafed in his time. He saw the House emptied of its ill-favoured tenants; he saw the workmen arrive and tear down the partitions of the mean little rooms and demolish the added floors; then he saw bricklayers, masons, and plasterers appear; scaffoldings were erected and, before long, he beheld his great Family House restored to its original outward form, resurrected in perfect structural repair. As for the interior, alas! Many of the lovely ceilings, most of the doors, the fountains, tesselated pavements, cupboards, and other household fittings had long since been pulled out and sold for what they would fetch, or burned for what firing they would provide.

Fortunately, at the time when I began my interior restorations, extensive demolitions were being carried out in the old quarters of Cairo, and essentials—especially of woodwork (doors, cupboards, panelling, screens etc.) of the period—were available as never before or since. In time, all in the House was restored or replaced, including the ceilings and two splendid contemporary fountains. In many cases such things as cupboards, doors, and other "fixtures" fitted into their prescribed spaces with an uncanny exactness, which gave one the feeling that all this was "meant." Only the two small bronze cannon that were reputed to have been mounted on the roof over the *hareem* and from there to have bombarded the Citadel, I was not able to replace.

Today, all is in order: the House, a happy House, is restored, reanimated with, as always, its vital centre at the tomb of its patron saint. This is still tended by an hereditary custodian from among the offspring of the Kretlis (none other than the son of our Sheikh) for, alas! the good old Sulaiman himself is no longer with us.

On the first day of Ragab in the year of the Hegira 1359 (July 26th, 1940) he died in his sleep at the age of over eighty years. To my regret, I was away from Cairo at the time.

I remembered afterwards with satisfaction how on my departure, as I drove off, I had looked back without apprehension and waved a hand to the Sheikh as he sat framed in the doorway under the little dome of the Saint's tomb which he had tended for seventy years and more. It turned out to be the last time I was to see that familiar figure squatting there on the ground in his accustomed attitude, bent over the Holy Book, the Koran, a cup of black coffee within reach. Absorbed in meditation, he did not see me as I drove past. That same night he was "gathered unto his fathers" and when I returned he was already buried.

Very real was my sorrow at this good man's passing, and my regret that I had not been able to pay my last tribute to so valued a friend by attending his funeral as he would have wished it, and setting my shoulder under his bier.[5]

Soon after my return, however, accompanied by his widow and two soldier sons, I visited his grave, a small vault within the enclosure of Sidi Gohara, close to the mosque of Sitt as-Sakina on the edge of the great Karafa burial-ground. There, as the custom is, I laid flowers and a palm branch on the plain stone catafalque that covered him.

Then it was they told me what a brave display the funeral procession had made—how many had been the mourners assembled from far and near—how numerous those who intoned the Koran and the women who followed, wailing and throwing dust on their heads—how eagerly the crowd had pressed forward to touch the rich shawl that covered the Sheikh or to help bear the burden of his *tabood*. I was told how the religious flags and banners—not only from the tomb of his own patron, Sidi Haroon, in our garden but also from the tombs of Saint Emery over the way and of Saints Howia and Hodari, all requisitioned for the occasion—had been carried in the burial procession, which looked like a *zaffa* (a ceremonial procession at a saint's *moolid*) rather than a funeral concourse, so they assured me. The body had been lifted out of the shell and lowered into its burial chamber near the mosque of Gohara, where it was laid on a bed of white sand, its face turned towards Mecca to await, in the tomb-chamber of his fathers, the two angels of death, Nunkir and Nakir.

Peace be unto him and the mercy of Allah and His blessing; may his presence enlighten the darkness and bring further benedictions upon the house of his family, the Bait al-Kretliya, and upon those who inhabit and visit it and upon its whole neighbourhood.

So much for Sheikh Sulaiman, the relater of these Legends; now it remains only to tell of their illustrator, the unique Abd al-Aziz Abdu, commonly known as *"Abu Shanab"* ("Father of Moustachios") on account of the glorious length of those he wears as may be seen from our photograph and from the self-portrait which appears in the headpiece to the Legends. He is still with us, I am glad to say; a tall, handsome man of middle age with a very fair complexion and keen reflective eyes heavily lashed.

He had for long been doing excellent work for me (repairing bronze antiques, engraving, making fittings and utensils, and much else) and as, at the time I was collecting the Legends from Sheikh Sulaiman, I had decided upon an addition to my copper dinner-service in the Bait al-Kretliya, the idea came to me of associating the Legends with the plates. I consulted Abd al-Aziz, who was enthusiastic. Thereafter, all I did was to read to him in Arabic each Legend as its turn came and to answer any questions he might wish to ask about it. He would then proceed with his circular composition and finally produce a full-sized drawing seven inches in diameter on paper. From this he made his engraving on the copper dinner-plate without consulting me further. Those dinner-plates are now in daily use and are kept in the service-room of the Bait al-Kretliya.

When Abd al-Aziz heard that I intended to make a book of the Legends with his designs as illustrations, he drew and engraved another design and presented the drawing and plate to me as a surprise backsheesh. This drawing I have included as a headpiece to the Legends. It is a portrait group of the three collaborators, each plainly labelled, Sheikh Sulaiman, Abd al-Aziz, and myself with my beloved dachshund "Fadl Effendi" ("Make yourself at home, Sir").

The last picture has nothing to do with the Legends. It is a design for yet another plate by Abd al-Aziz which I commissioned from him to commemorate a visit I paid, accompanied by my twin Brother, to an island at Aswan which I had bought hoping to build a small house on it: a project that unfortunately had to be abandoned. I have reproduced the drawing here as a tailpiece to the Legends because it introduces my twin Brother, who so often stayed with me at the Bait al-Kretliya, and because it completes the set of sixteen designs by Abd al-Aziz.

As he finished each plate, the Artist brought it along for my inspection and was always delighted at the obvious pleasure which his originality and the excellence of his work gave me.

I feel that the form of illustration which Abd al-Aziz has employed could not have been improved upon justly to convey the sense, feeling, and atmosphere of the following folk and Koranic legends. In my opinion they can stand on their own merits as examples of folk-art entirely free from European influence, and they derive a certain importance from the fact that, alas! this form of ingenious and unstudied native art is rapidly dying out. For that reason, amongst others, I am particularly glad to have been able to perpetuate these drawings and to express my appreciation of them and their creator.

Now let me close this Introduction with the beautiful words of the Koran:

"O God, make my labour to be approved and my sin forgiven, and my works accepted, merchandise that shall not perish..."

The Bait al-Kretliya, Cairo, 1943

The Artist

Notes

1. For the history of the House and the origins of its present name, see Note 1 to the Sixth Legend.
2. See the Twelfth Legend.
3. *Mashallah*, literally "What Allah Wishes," is an expression much used and with a subtle variety of meanings, the most common being to avert the evil eye after praising somebody or something. Then it means "but nevertheless as Allah wills it."
4. See Note 5 to the Ninth Legend.
5. The dead in Egypt are borne to the grave shoulder-high in an open *tabood* (bier) covered over with a Cashmere shawl.

The House of the Cretan Woman

by Nicholas Warner

We saw the Bait al-Kritliya; the West,
Where its doors close, is a forgotten land;
It was a house Mahomet might have blest,
But for the hospitable wines at hand.
Damascus, Trebizond, and Samarkand
Had furnished it: what other towns as well
I know not, but beyond Arabia's sand
Their towers stood. Soft in this citadel
Of ancient Eastern things a dreaming fountain fell.

From "A Journey" by Lord Dunsany[1]

The Bait al-Kretliya—the House of the Cretan Woman—was originally not one house, but two. Located on either side of an alley leading into the mosque of Ibn Tulun, the houses were linked at an unknown point in their history by a high-level bridge. Both have their rooms arranged around courtyards that back onto the outer wall of the mosque. One room even has windows that peer through the crenellations that crown this wall. Although they are the only surviving houses today that share such a close relationship with the mosque, this was not always the case. Until a large scale urban clearance operation was carried out in the 1920s by the Department of Antiquities, the mosque had many structures attached to its outer walls, most of them houses. These houses belonged to a prosperous community that lived in densely packed quarters separated by narrow alleyways. The demolitions were carried out in order to isolate the mosque from its context. This was believed to be necessary in accordance with the historic importance of the mosque as the primary survival of the city that was constructed here by Ahmad Ibn Tulun in the ninth century. The Bait al-Kretliya and its counterpart were spared from demolition because of their intrinsic artistic interest. They were thus, in their own turn, separated from the urban fabric in which they were embedded. This process required a considerable amount of reconstruction of

17

the perimeter walls of the two houses, which was carried out in the Islamic style. Despite this rebuilding, all the most significant spaces within the houses are original, as is their close topographic relationship to the mosque. Today, the passage between the houses is the last surviving fragment that gives us an idea of how the mosque was approached from the city through one of the many doorways located in its outer wall.

The immediate physical proximity of the house to the mosque is paralleled by a mythic connection that is recorded in the collection of popular legends presented in this book. Some have echoes in the chronicles of the historians who described the mosque, its construction, and various restorations. Some are transmutations of well-known sections of the Qur'an. Others reflect common Egyptian folkloric themes

The Mosque of Ibn Tulun with the House of the Cretan Woman at its southeast corner

that are part of the oral tradition and rarely set down. The sacred nature of the site, a rocky outcrop known as the Gebel Yashkur, which was used as a cemetery before the mosque was built, lent itself to such interpretations. The unique value of the legends derives from the union of the tangible world of architecture with the intangible realm of association. Too often the one survives without the other, but when seen together they reinforce our understanding of a place and its continuity with the past.

The two houses were both constructed during the period of the Ottoman domination of Egypt. This began when Sultan Selim I (known as 'the Grim') invaded the country in 1517 and defeated the Mamluks, a military élite that had ruled for the preceding 250 years. The Bait al-Kretliya is the house that is located on the right-hand side of the alley facing the mosque of Ibn Tulun, and is datable from in situ inscriptions as the foundation of one Muhammad Hagg Salim in 1631. Its counterpart across the alley has been attributed to the sixteenth century on stylistic grounds. The original owners of the houses were probably wealthy merchants who traded in coffee or spices. The current names of the two properties—the Bait al-Kretliya and the Bait Amna bint Salim (house of Amna the daughter of Salim)—are derived from two women who were more recent owners.

The form and decoration of the buildings, however, owe more to local precedents than any models imported from Ottoman Turkey. The earlier Mamluk period in Egypt had established most architectural typologies in Cairo, and lent them great sophistication and distinction. Elaborate doorways, spacious loggias, tripartite reception rooms, inlaid marble fountains, coffered and painted wooden ceilings, delicate surface treatments, and projecting wooden latticed windows (known as *mashrabiya*) can all be found in houses from this time and even earlier. But whereas the earlier houses are vast in their scale, later derivatives are reduced to more intimate proportions. There is a compression of the essential building elements to suit less lavish circumstances and clients with different needs: merchants rather than princes. Cairo was, since the inception of al-Fustat (the first Arab city in Egypt) in the seventh century, a great trading center by virtue of its geographic location at the apex of the Nile Delta and the head of desert caravan routes. It was only natural for those who grew rich by their trade to display their wealth in the architecture of their homes.

All of the characteristic elements of such houses mentioned above can be found in the Bait al-Kretliya, starting with the elements used in construction. As in much Islamic domestic architecture, greater emphasis is placed on the interiors than the exteriors in terms of spatial elaboration and embellishment. The plain façades, both internal and external, are built of dressed limestone, with decoration confined to significant structural components or openings. Such decoration takes the form of carved stone banding, or facetted geometric patterns (known as *muqarnas* or 'stalactites'). Both of these treatments have the effect of bringing depth and shadow to the surface of an otherwise blank façade. Occasionally, as on the corner of the *sabil*, or drinking fountain, that is part of the Bait al-Kretliya, a particular feature is highlighted by its decorative treatment: in this case the engaged stone column on the corner of the *sabil* has an interlocking geometric design carved upon it. Another example is the inner entrance to the same house, which is recessed beneath a tall trefoil hood and has panels of marble inlaid within it in geometric patterns. The inner courtyards of both houses are approached by dog-legged, or baffled, corridors. These deny any direct access to the interiors, and have places for caretakers or doorkeepers to stand guard. The ground floor is occupied by rooms that were originally used for storage, or by the servants of the house. Both houses have loggias on their first floor (known as a *maq'ad* or a 'place for sitting'). The example in the Bait al-Kretliya is more representative of this architectural element in that it is composed of a pair of pointed arches that rest at their center on a single reused antique column and capital. The loggia of the house of Amna bint Salim possesses only a single arch. Such spaces functioned as outdoor reception rooms, where the owner of the house would sit, entertain, and supervise activities taking place in the courtyard he overlooked. In Cairo, these loggias are almost invariably oriented to the northwest in order to take advantage of the prevailing wind that brings relief from the desert heat.

Within each house are reception rooms that are long and extremely tall. They follow the classic Cairene model of spatial division in which the room is divided into three sections: the central portion being lower than the areas to either side, which are used for sitting (the *qa'a*). The ceilings in these rooms are of wood painted with floral motifs and are bordered with inscriptions. In one room, this central

area is further ornamented by a large polychrome inlaid marble fountain. Marble is a material that is usually reserved for elements of the building that relate to water: decorative marble 'mantelpieces' can be seen where ewers and basins were kept for the

The southeast corner of the courtyard

use of the household. Water is also behind the name for one of the most distinctive features of the traditional Cairene house: the projecting bay window fabricated from turned-wood screens in a plethora of different designs. These are known by the generic name of *mashrabiya*, which is literally translated as 'a place for drinking.' This is because drinking water was placed in small, porous earthenware jars in these windows, where they caught the breeze, which cooled the water by evaporation. The windows also have the effect of filtering the glare from outside, giving a softer dappled light to the interior.

The Bait al-Kretliya today is furnished in an 'oriental' mode, with a large number of objects occupying every space. This does not give an accurate picture of how such a house would traditionally have been fitted out. Rooms were used by the household dependent on climate: some rooms for summer and others for winter. This meant that the 'furnishings' for each room were portable, and were stored in cupboards located around the perimeter of each room until such time as they were required. No room had a particular function ascribed to it, as is the case today in the west; rather each room could be the receptacle for a variety of activities. Another important way in which houses were spatially divided was by gender. The women lived in relative seclusion, unseen except by their families and close friends, while their menfolk mediated with the world outside and with visitors to the house. The world of the women is known as the *haramlik*, while that of the men is the *salamlik*. Sometimes women in the former could observe, without being seen themselves, events taking place in the latter from a screened balcony or other secret hiding place. One of the large reception rooms in the House of Amna bint Salim preserves just such an arrangement.

In addition to having the standard elements of

The loggia and decorated entrance in the courtyard of the Bait al-Kretliya

The main *qaʻa* of the Bait Amna bint Salim

The main *qaʻa* of the Bait al-Kretliya

domestic architecture described above, the Bait al-Kretliya also has some unusual features. In one courtyard there is a well. Well water in Cairo is generally not potable, being salty and brackish, so it would have been used for watering animals or for cleaning. This well, however, is credited with magical powers and is known as the 'Well of the Bats' *(Bir al-Watawit)*. It features in several of the legends that are recounted here. The connection between dark, watery places and the supernatural

is well attested, since bathrooms, wells, and cisterns are traditionally the haunt of the *djinn*, a supernatural spirit with the capacity for both good and evil.

Another water feature attached to the house is the *sabil*, or public drinking fountain. Such a fountain would have been constructed originally as an act of charity to supply a particular neighborhood with drinking water. The water was offered in basins behind two large bronze window grilles, to

Interior of the *harem* room

which were chained brass drinking mugs. The thirsty dipped these mugs into the basins and drank. A *sabil* was usually built with a *kuttab*, or Qur'anic school, above it, which provided a basic education for orphans. This is also true for the Bait al-Kretliya, which is extremely unusual in having a *sabil-kuttab* attached to it, since these structures are normally found attached to mosques or built as independent charitable foundations. Beneath the *sabil* is an enormous cistern, where water would have been stored ready for distribution after it had been painstakingly brought from the Nile by water-carriers or animals. Another remarkable feature of the house is the small domed tomb attached to one corner. This ancient tomb was substantially rebuilt at the time of the remodeling of the exterior of the building in the 1930s, and is ascribed to Sidi Haroun, a descendent of the Prophet Muhammad, which confers further mystique upon the house.

The Well of the Bats

Interior of the *sabil*

Gayer-Anderson made several embellishments to the interior of the house when it was converted into first his private residence and subsequently his eponymous museum. The first of these was a roof garden with turned-wood screens. Also on the top floor of the house are a series of themed rooms that include the Muhammad 'Ali period room and the Damascus Room. The latter is a rebuilt room from a seventeenth-century Syrian house, disassembled and imported into Egypt. Gayer-Anderson also furnished the house with his extraordinary and eclectic collection of artifacts, which can be admired to this day. These include pharaonic relief fragments and mummy cases, Coptic textiles and tombstones, and modern European paintings and objets d'art. Pride of place goes, as is fitting, to the Islamic material, which ranges from begging bowls used by Sufis to engraved ostrich eggs, taking in the worlds of

The Muhammad 'Ali Room

ceramics, metalwork, textiles, manuscripts, and glass on the way. It is a tribute to Gayer-Anderson that at no point does the display inhibit one's appreciation of the complex and intriguing architecture of the original building. Rather, this diversity of objects seems to complement both the richness of the house and the legends that have surrounded it for hundreds of years.

Note

1. Edward John Moreton Drax Plunkett, the 18th Baron Dunsany (1878–1957), was a noted poet and playwright who derived much of his inspiration from mythological and fantastic themes. He most probably visited the Bait al-Kretliya in the late 1930s. This quotation and the photographs that illustrate this essay are reproduced from the first edition of *The Legends of the Bait al-Kretliya*.

The
Legends

A Note on the Illustrations

The original illustrations of the Legends of the House of the Cretan Woman by Abd al-Aziz Abdu are bound in an album now in the possession of the Victoria and Albert Museum in London. Those familiar with Persian miniature painting will notice the repetition of certain motifs that are well known from this genre. This suggests a familiarity on the part of the artist with such material. The artist has also adopted the practice of including several incidents from each Legend, or occasionally a scene from a different but related Legend, in the same illustration.

For this edition of the Legends, the illustrations have all been redrawn by the author's grandson, Theo Gayer-Anderson. While they remain the same as the originals in composition, certain enhancements have been made for the sake of the clarity of the images. These apply particularly to the decorative treatment of objects and the faces of the protagonists. The inclusion of color in the illustrations has also made them easier to 'read.'

The backgrounds to almost all the illustrations have four significant motifs in common. Three of these are architectural elements, and are labeled in Arabic: "the Tomb of Haroun" (a small building with a dome), "the Mosque of Ibn Tulun" (represented by its distinctive minaret), and "the Bait al-Kretliya" (with windows and an arched doorway). The fourth motif, which is not labeled, is a large pointed tree. This tree is part of the family crest of Gayer-Anderson, which can also be seen on several cupboards and doors in the Bait al-Kretliya. The reason for the inclusion of this device is that the tree represents the person of Gayer-Anderson historically

The Collaborators

Translation of the inscriptions: "Done in Cairo by order of the owner of the Bait al-Kretliya, Gayer-Anderson Bey, in the year 1358 Hegira. The Sheikh Sulaiman al-Kretli, the Owner and his dog 'Fadl Effendi', and the Artist Abd al-Aziz Abdu." On the sleeves, left to right, are the names of the Artist, Author, and Sheikh. On the buildings are their names.

throughout the Legends, just as Sidi Haroun, Ahmad Ibn Tulun, and the Kretli family are represented by their buildings.

Each illustration has a principal inscription in Arabic that runs around its border, as well as labels for the people and buildings that are a part of the Legend. These inscriptions and labels are all in colloquial, not classical, Arabic. An English translation of all the inscriptions, except for the routine architectural labelings mentioned above, is given for each illustration.

N.W.

The First Legend

The Landing of Noah's Ark

In the Name of God, the Compassionate, the Merciful. And now, Oh honoured friend, I shall begin these Legends of the Bait al-Kretliya, the ancient House of my Family, with four tales which concern a time long before the building of that House or of the great Mosque of Ahmad Ibn Tulun. None the less, the four Legends with which I shall commence make as it were a foundation on which to build the later Legends. They concern the House and the great Mosque very closely, for they tell of the sacred ground on which those buildings are erected: the Gebel Yashkur—'The Hill of Thanksgiving'—and how in the earliest times it, and its neighbourhood, became so blessed and sanctified. And let me inform you now that there is no doubt whatever but that it was here all of the marvellous events took place of which these four Legends tell, and not at any other places as is sometimes erroneously maintained, for the history of each of them is recounted not only in the Koran but also in your Sacred Books so that any who wish may read of them therein.[1]

Know then that the blessed hill, the Gebel Yashkur, on which the Bait al-Kretliya and the great Mosque of Ibn Tulun are built, was at one time the highest in Egypt, loftier far than it now is, rising up to a considerable peak.

It was on this peak then—and not on Mount Ararat as some have supposed—that the Blessed Ark came to rest after the Flood had subsided,[2] and here *Sidna* (our Master), Noah, and his sons and their women stepped forth with every kind of beast, two by two, male and female, to replenish the earth, for had not God said, 'Oh Noah! Disembark with peace from Us and with blessings on thee and on all peoples to be born from those that are with thee.'[3]

Translation of the inscriptions: "The Bait al-Kretliya, near the Mosque of Ibn Tulun, in Cairo. Drawn by Abd al-Aziz Abdu for His Excellency Gayer-Anderson Bey." On the canopy of the Ark, "Noah's Boat." Under the Ark, "The Mountain of Yashkur."

You will recall that when Father Noah, after the revelation of Allah, was building his Ark, they that passed by jeered at the Prophet, and taunted him, saying, 'To what end make ye such a great vessel?'— but he answered them not and only went on with his work to its finish, so that soon thereafter all they that had mocked him, together with the rest of that vile generation, were drowned in the Deluge.

Only Noah, as I have said, together with his wife and his sons and their wives, was saved, and landed from the Ark here on the Gebel Yashkur to set up the first city of Cairo—that is, the first after the Flood, for the Pharaohs had built here before then and had hewn a deep pit through the rock of the Gebel as Joseph, Jacob's son, did at the Citadel while he sojourned in Egypt[4] and it was into this pit, which is now the *'Beer al-Watawit'* ('Well of the Bats') in the court of the Bait al-Kretliya, that the last of the Deluge subsided, for had not God said, 'Oh Earth! Swallow up thy waters. Oh Heaven, cease!' Ever since then this has been counted a holy well, and about it I shall have more to relate anon.

Now, when the great Ibn Tulun came to build his mosque, Noah's Ark was still stranded high and dry here on Mount Yashkur, a record of our good master Noah's landing and an undoubted proof that the Ark rested here after the Flood in days long since gone by, for such was God's will.

Notes

1. Throughout these tales much naïve historical and geographical confusion exists, as well as general inaccuracy, as the reader will doubtless observe.

2. The Koran says: 'And the water abated, and the decree was fulfilled, and the Ark rested upon al-Judi.' There is no indication, however, as to where 'the hill al-Judi' is or was.

3. This and many following quotations are from the Koran. Such quotations are frequent and apposite in the speech of the pious, many of whom know most of the Koran or even the whole of it by heart.

Those who do so are not infrequently blind and illiterate (quite unable either to read or to write).

4. 'Joseph's Well' (Beer Yusef) at the Citadel is popularly supposed to have been made by Joseph, the aforesaid son of Jacob. As a matter of fact it was Yusef (Joseph) Salah ad-Din (the famous "Saladin," the Saracen Crusader and friendly foe of Richard Coeur de Lion) who sank it in the 12th century A.D. to supply his stronghold, the Citadel, with water. He also built the walls of Cairo.

The Second Legend

Abraham's Sacrifice

In the Name of God, the Compassionate, the Merciful. Oh my honoured Master, I have told you how the Ark came to rest here on the Gebel Yashkur and how *Sidna* Noah stepped down with two of each kind to re-people the earth and this by itself might well account for the hill being called 'Blessed' and 'Holy' and 'Sanctified' as it often is, but I have not as yet explained why the hill is called Yashkur, 'a place of thanksgiving.' Know then that this is because long ago, in order to try him, the Lord appeared thrice in his dreams unto Ibraheem (Abraham), who had first been a pagan but came to know God and to be called His good friend.

Thrice God appeared to Ibraheem bidding him slay his beloved son Ismail (Ishmael) as a sacrifice, to which the lad nobly consented,[1] for when his father reported his vision to Ismail, the boy boldly replied, 'Do as thou art commanded Oh my Father.' There-

after he was laid 'prostrate on his face' and, all being made ready, Ibraheem, according to some, drew his knife with all his strength across the lad's throat but without any result, for the knife refused to cut, and thereat came the voice of reprieve while from above an angel descended, bearing with him a ram, and this Ibraheem slew in his son's stead. So the angel brought rejoicing unto him who till then had sorrowed, and Ibraheem thanked Allah for His mercy.

That is how and why they named the place 'The Hill of Thanksgiving' and where the altar was set—there to the west of the mosque of Ibn Tulun—they built a high citadel and called it, as it is still called, the *Qal'at al-Kabsh*, (the Fort of the Ram),[2] a stronghold the walls of which have long since fallen into ruin.

So it is that through the mercy of God grief may be turned into joy and what seemeth affliction prove but a trial of fortitude.

Translation of the inscriptions: "Drawn by Abd al-Aziz Abdu the Artist. On the hill of Yashkur, on which the Bait al-Kretliya is now built, when Sidna Ibraheem was about to sacrifice his son, Ishaq, God redeemed him with a ram, hence the place is known as 'The Fortress of the Ram'." On the four central figures, left to right, "Ibraheem," "Ishaq," "The Ram," and "Gibriel."

Notes

1. According to the Koran it was Ishmael and not Isaac, as in the Bible story, who was the proffered sacrifice in this episode. The miracle is also reputed to have happened at the Dome of the Rock in Jerusalem, but in the Koran it is stated to have occurred in the valley of Mina near Mecca. It will be noted that in the Koranic version the ram was not found 'caught in a thicket' as in the Biblical story but was brought down from heaven by an angel. Ismail, son of Hagar, the progenitor of the Arabian race, was at this time a lad of thirteen, a 'meek youth' yet resolute.

2. Lane-Poole speaks of the *Qal'at al-Kabsh* as 'the place by the hill of Yashkur, known as 'The Castle of the Ram'.' He relates how it was built 'probably on an ancient foundation' in 1245 A.D. and used as a royal palace. Rebuilt in 1323 A.D., it became the residence of the Emir Sargitmish, whose beautiful mosque-tomb stands close by. Finally, the place became humble tenement dwellings. Little more than a hundred years ago its massive ruins were conspicuous, but now nothing remains above ground but a scarp faced with huge blocks of stone that may be seen best from below, off the Sharia Hodari.

The Third Legend

The Confounding
of Pharaoh's Magicians[1]

In the Name of God, the Compassionate, the Merciful. Oh beloved friend, let me now tell of the third redoubtable happening in ancient days which added to the sanctity of this neighbourhood, for it took place on the Gebel Yashkur at the Mastaba al-Faraun, which was then a vast palace, the seat of the Pharaohs, Kings of Egypt at that early time, and even now parts of its foundations can still be seen.[2]

What I shall tell you concerns one of the episodes of that master magician, the Prophet *Sidna* Moosa, and how, at the challenge of the Pharaoh (one of that impious line of monarchs), he came to their palace. There, while the king and his wazirs looked down from the royal kiosk, *Sidna* Moosa, standing below, faced the chief magicians of Egypt, between whom and this man of God there existed a great and bitter rivalry.

By the grace of God, the Prophet confounded them all and it so happened that after many and remarkable trials of cunning and craft, in each of which Pharaoh's people were completely outwitted, as a final test of their magic they threw down their rods upon the ground whereat by an evil enchantment those rods turned into serpents. By this piece of sorcery they thought completely to confound the great Prophet but, nothing daunted, he in his turn at once cast down *his* staff upon the ground, whereupon it became a fiery dragon which not only consumed the serpents of Pharaoh's magicians but also devoured their masters. At this, the king admitted that *Sidna* Moosa was mightier than any of his magicians, and he was much troubled and disconcerted, for is it not written in the Koran—'verily on that day when the hour (of Judgment) hath come, the people of Pharaoh shall be introduced to the severest punishments.'[3]

Translation of the inscriptions: "On this hill of Yashkur God appeared to our Master Moosa in a burning fire, and near this place Moosa came before Pharaoh and threw down his staff as a challenge and it turned into a dragon which swallowed up the ten staves which Pharaoh's magicians had thrown down, for which reason the place where this miracle happened is known as Pharaoh's Mastaba." On the figures, left to right, "Moosa," "Pharaoh," "Magician." On the kiosk "Pharaoh's Mastaba."

41

Notes

1. According to the Koran, Moses was commanded to 'go unto Pharaoh for he is excessively impious' with 'nine signs from God,' and convert him. A meeting and long argument followed, and then a trial of magical power was arranged between the Pharaoh's magicians on the one side and Moses and Aaron on the other. In this the former were entirely confounded, baffled, and discomfited as here described. 'We believe in the God of Moosa,' they cried at last. 'You dare to believe before I have given you permission?' stormed the despotic Pharaoh, and so enraged was he that the Prophet of God thought it best 'to go forth from Egypt by night,' and this he did. Neither Moslem nor Jew wastes much love on the Pharaohs.

2. I have visited the site of this *Mastaba* and no such remains are now to be seen. It is indeed unlikely that any Pharaonic palace ever stood here. What doubtless gave rise to the legend was the presence of a large granite sarcophagus which appears, surrounded by fine buildings, in the illustrations to some early travel books on Egypt (Mayer's, etc.) This was the sarcophagus of a lady of the 17th dynasty and is now in the British Museum. The place was believed to be haunted by jinn—mostly benevolent—who would turn whatever was brought there to gold if you knew the right formula, but no one ever did know that formula. There seems always to have been an insurmountable 'if' in these get-rich-quick matters.

3. Koran—Surat Ghafir (v. 45.)

The Fourth Legend

The Burning Bush

In the Name of God, the Compassionate, the Merciful. And now, Oh beloved Brother, let me tell of the fourth of those miraculous events which took place upon this hill of Yashkur[1] and which ensure its four-fold blessedness, its renown, and good name, for it was here that *Rabbuna* ('God Almighty' or 'The Almighty') appeared unto *Sidna* Moosa as a bright flame out of a bush and spake to the Prophet. God bless and preserve him.[2]

Know then that in those days, thousands of years ago, the face of our earth was not as it now is in these parts; for though Cairo was already a large city wherein dwelt the Pharaohs and the Pashas of old among their great temples and palaces, and surrounded by priests of pagan belief worshipping beasts, the city did not include this sacred hill of Yashkur, which then stood outside its walls as a green eminence covered over with bushes, whereon the flocks grazed.

Upon it *Sidna* Moosa, having come to Egypt for the first time, pitched his tent. One blessed day he was looking out from the door of his tent when, lo and behold, he perceived a bush not far off standing amongst all the rest, and it appeared to be on fire, for flames were issuing from its centre with such brilliance that he dared not keep his eyes upon it; yet though it burned thus vividly, no smoke came from it; and though it was so brightly ablaze, it was not consumed; and though one might have expected a great warmth to come from such a conflagration, there was no heat apparent, for birds circled about it and sang in its branches while above it angels hovered in the sky.

Then *Sidna* Moosa, gathering his *abaya* (outer garment) about him, drew on his sandals in great haste and went forth, running up to the place where the bush was burning. In the greatest amazement he ran, for he realised this to be no common event.

And as he drew near a voice spake from that burning bush, saying, 'Oh Moosa, verily I am Allah thy God. Put the sandals from off thy feet for thou standest upon holy ground.' And that holy ground whereon the bush burned was this very place where later Ahmad Ibn Tulun built his great Mosque.

On hearing the words of God, *Sidna* Moosa, casting off his sandals, fell upon his face and lay there prostrate while the Voice spake again, saying, 'Blessed be He who is in the fire and whosoever is about it,' and again, 'Oh Moosa, I am thy God.'³ And

after a long time, when the Prophet dared to look up again, behold, the vision was gone and there was silence; nor was the bush consumed; nor were there any signs of fire about it.

This miraculous happening it is, Oh my beloved friend, that imparts more than all else great sanctity to the hill whereon we stand, the Gebel Yashkur, 'The Hill of Thanksgiving.' For it was here and thus that *Rabbuna* made himself known to the Prophet. It was later that he treated with God and had the tablets of the Law from him.

Notes

1. 'Yashkur … was a sure place for prayer to be answered,' says Lane-Poole, 'since it was believed to be the spot where Moses had converse with Jehovah.' More generally however this miracle is said to have taken place in Sinai while the Prophet was journeying on his way to Egypt. The Koranic account of this superlative event speaks of the place as Tawa by name, but none know where Tawa was or is.

2. Some say that the bush concerned was not 'flaming' in the sense of giving off flames but in full bloom or in brilliant green leaf, for in speaking of a plant in full bloom the Arabs often use the word 'flaming' or 'burning' just as we do.

3. The Koranic differs from the Biblical account of this event in that here the Prophet makes no demand to behold the Almighty (*vide* Exodus XXXIII, verses 18–23). The Prophet and Ali had commune with God in heaven.

The Fifth Legend

Ahmad Ibn Tulun Builds His Mosque[1]

In the Name of God, the Compassionate, the Merciful. Here, Oh my honoured friend, is yet another Legend which, though it does not tell directly of the Bait al-Kretliya, closely concerns it, for it deals with the actual raising, by Ahmad Ibn Tulun, of the great Mosque on to which our House is built in such a manner that it may with truth be considered to constitute part of that sacred edifice.

Know then that when the great Sultan Ahmad Ibn Tulun, may God bless and pity him, came to build his Mosque in Egypt in the early days of the Hegira, he was anxious to place it on as commanding and holy a site as might be. After consulting the wise men of Cairo, therefore, he chose the Gebel Yashkur as its situation for, as I have told you, that was in those days the highest hill in Egypt, far higher than it is now; and indeed, even now, only the eminence on

which Yusef Salah ad-Din, the conqueror, built his Citadel, and the hills of Muqattam beyond it, are higher. It was, moreover, by far the most blessed and holy locality by reason of those four sacred events which I have related. Indeed, this ground—as that of al-Haram as-Shareef, the honoured enclosure at Jerusalem—was as holy a spot as could be found, not only in Egypt but far and wide, and peopled by many good spirits.[2] Since then, its honour and sanctity have been ever increased, both by the building of the great and holy Mosque and by the bones of the many blessed that have since then been interred here-abouts, amongst them those of our honoured Imam as-Shafii, that saintly leader of Islam.[3]

In order to level the site which he had chosen, the Sultan shore off the whole top of the Gebel Yashkur and, having reduced it to the height it is now, he set the foundation of his Mosque upon the living rock so

Translation of the inscriptions: "Here, in the year 263 Hegira, the generous Sultan Ahmad Ibn Tulun came and worked with his own hands and built his Mosque, which is still standing; and he built around it his palace and the fortress of al-Qataii, the remains of which disappeared a long time ago." On the central figure above, "The Sultan Ahmad Ibn Tulun builds with his own hands."

The Sixth Legend

The House Is Built[1]

In the Name of God, the Compassionate, the Merciful. And now, Oh well beloved friend, having laid the foundations of the Legends of the Bait al-Kretliya which are to follow, by recounting to you the four tales of ancient times which prove how sanctified and blessed is the ground on which the House and the great Mosque are built, and that last Legend which tells of the building of the Mosque itself, let me begin the Legends which are directly concerned with the Bait al-Kretliya, the ancient dwelling of my Family, thus keeping all in its proper order. Hear then, Oh honoured friend, how my forbears first came to build the House at the same time as the great Sultan Ibn Tulun was constructing his Mosque and Palace in this locality, or shortly thereafter.

My forbear also was at pains to dig its foundations down to the living rock, whereon they raised its thick walls and so, like the mosque, this house has remained ever since, undisturbed by time, or flood, or by earthquakes which have done much to destroy other ancient buildings, cracking old walls and shaking minarets to the ground.[2]

They that laid the plan of the house set it about the Beer al-Watawit (The Well of the Bats)[3] so that this deep and miraculous pit, which has been here since before the days of the Flood, should be in its midst surrounded on all sides by the high walls of the courtyard. This they did, it is said, at the request of the King of the Jinn, the Sultan al-Watawit—who dwells in a palace in the depths of the well—so that he might be protected and left in peace there while his seven fair daughters lie asleep amid his priceless treasure, as to which I shall have more to relate anon.

Translation of the inscriptions: "Here, in the year 1041 Hegira, the Hagg Mohammed, son of the late Hagg Saleem, son of the late Hagg Galmam, built this House near the door of the Mosque of Ibn Tulun, and finally the ownership of this House was transferred to a Lady from the Island of Crete and since then it has been known as the Bait al-Kretliya." Below the female figure left top, "It was owned by a Lady from the Island of Crete." On the figure to the right top, "The Hagg Galmam."

Indeed, they say that the King of the Jinn, out of his riches, supplied all that my forbears required to build and embellish the House, and that for long thereafter he and they remained good friends and in league the one with the other. Certain it is that the Kretlis never were short of money until, as I shall tell you in due course, a certain foolish woman threw away their store of gold. Ever since then our family, from being rich and esteemed, has fallen on needy days and now stands at God's door to seek His protection.

I shall tell you also how, at one corner of the house, a dome[4] came to be built in Fatimite days to receive the holy remains of our master Haroon, son of Husein, whose servant and guardian I have the honour to be—as were my fathers before me—and in whose Tomb I now live. At another corner a *sabeel* with a *kuttab* (school for boys) above it was erected as part of the house, with two great bronze grilles opening South and West on to the lane that leads to the main door of the Mosque so that worshippers coming and going might quench their thirst[5] and refresh themselves and praise Allah.

The Bait al-Kretliya, when finished, was tall, strong, and well-built of stone as you see it today. Indeed, they say that it was so fine that in his day it caught the eye and excited the envy of no less a person than the Pasha of Egypt, The great Mohammed Ali himself (1769-1858), who forthwith gave orders that the top storey be demolished so as to bring this house down to the level of the other great ones nearby.

Some maintain, moreover, that at this time the Kretlis, like many more Mameluke Beys, were at enmity with, and intriguing against, the Pasha and that, having built a fort on the roof over the *hareem* and

mounted two cannon on it, they kept dropping round-shot at intervals into the Citadel in so cunning a manner that the Viceroy could not determine from whence they came, nor would perhaps have found out had not the fact been betrayed by one who bore ill will against my Family. The very day after that betrayal, the Pasha descended in wrath and caused the fort to be torn down and its two cannon carried away; indeed it is said he would have demolished the whole house in his anger had not my mother—who was alone, for her husband and all his armed men had, of necessity, fled—spoken to the Pasha so fair that he was won over, and left the place undestroyed and my people still in possession. The praise be to Allah.[6]

In the good old days the Kretlis kept many retainers, and many guests came to stay in the house, these being lodged and entertained in the great *salamlik,* entered across the lane that leads to the Mosque, the Atfit al-Gama. The mistress of the house, her daughters, servants, and female visitors, entered the family portion of the house through the great eastern door that gives on to the street which is called 'The Way to the Well of the Bats,' our magical well in the courtyard below, and passing up the short hidden stair came to the *hareem* on the first floor. Next to this women's apartment at the head of the stairs is a small room we called the *khasna* or safe-place: it was there that our babies were born. I first saw the light in that room, and my fathers before me, for all our women gave birth in this little chamber, according to custom.[7]

On the ground floor, opening into the courtyard, the rooms were used by the men servants to sleep in or for store places, and in one of these there was a mill in which corn for the house was ground, and they say that this mill was used by the French when Bonaparte came into Egypt. A passage once ran from the house under the Mosque, at the end of which there lies a hoard of gold, all that remains of the treasure with which Ibn Tulun completed his building. To discover this wealth, as likewise the treasure in the Well of the Bats about which I shall tell you later, has been the ambition of many in these parts, but so far no one has succeeded. Yea, verily 'all that is with you passeth away but that which is with God abideth.'

This is indeed a privileged house for not only has it on its premises that well—in the depths of which there dwells the benign King of the Jinn—but it also harbours a benevolent serpent, of which I shall tell next, which safeguards the place: but above all, the House is blessed in sheltering a saint's body, which rests here in our midst, bringing peace and well-being to all who inhabit the place so that it cannot be haunted by ghoul or *afreet,* as it certainly would be were it not for such blessed protection. 'In God we take refuge from all the unholy.'8

Notes

1. In this story it should be remembered that these are the reminiscences of an old man whose fathers—as well as himself—were born, bred, and lived their lives in this house so that traditions and customs embodied in the following Legends are centred around it. As I have already said, the Sheikh's dates, and his placing of historical events which arise from time to time in these tales, are always unreliable and 'facts' often fabulous; thus, despite what he tells us in all good faith, the Mosque of Ibn Tulun was not contemporary with the Bait al-Kretliya but preceded it by at least six centuries. Nor was the house originally founded and possessed by his family but by another, as testified by the inscription that runs round the beautiful ceilings of both the *maq'ad* and *sabeel* and which reads as follows:

'This blessed *maq'ad* (or *sabeel*) was built by the favour of God and with His assistance by the Hagg Mohammed, son of the deceased Hagg Salem, son of the deceased Hagg Galmam, and was finished in the year forty after the thousand of the Hegira' (A.H. 1040 or A.D. 1641). The name Galmam is unusual and difficult to assign; it seems to be possibly Arab, of the same genre as Lamlum which we have in Egypt, or perhaps Turkoman. Its derivation from the French Guillaume (William) has also been suggested, but French Mamelukes were very uncommon. About the end of the 18th century or the beginning of the 19th, the House appears to have come into the possession of a lady from Crete after whom it has ever since been called Bait al-Kretliya, 'the House of the Cretan Lady,' although it could equally well mean 'the house of the Cretan Family,' a Family now familiarly known as the Kretlis, of which Sheikh Sulaiman was a direct descendant.

2. The top of Gebel Yashkur was shorn off, and a Christian cemetery removed, to make room for the Mosque of Ibn Tulun. Nowhere does the rock appear to be more than a few feet from the surface, as was made plain by the air-raid shelter trenches which were recently dug (1940) on the grass slope to the east of the House and Mosque.

3. The Arabic for 'bat' is 'witwat,' plural 'watawit,' hence 'The Well of the Bats,' but this name is doubtless connected with the fact that the '*Sultan al-Watawit*' (Sultan of the Bats), who will be mentioned shortly, lives in a palace at the bottom of this magic well. He is indeed a powerful potentate, for he is also 'King of the Jinn.'

4. A 'dome' (*qubba*) has become the generic name for a tomb. Wherever you see a dome in Old Cairo there will be a catafalque, a burial, under it.

5. The *sabeel* is quite unique in the whole of Cairo, being the only one installed in a private house, and yet of sufficient size and beauty of construction to rank with most public examples in this city. These latter are nearly always combined with a *kuttab*, which is invariably situated above the fountain room: this was doubtless once the case here. As stated elsewhere, the inscription that runs round its highly ornate ceiling is the same as that round the *maq'ad*.

6. The intrigue and enmity among the Mameluke Beys themselves, and displayed against the reigning house, led to a wholesale assassination, or purge, in 1811 by Mohammed Ali. A 'fort' (more exactly a gun emplacement), such as is described here, might well have been placed over the *hareem*, which is built upon four massive columns of masonry.

7. The smallest and most airless room or closet was generally reserved for this purpose in those days, much as was then the custom in Europe also.

8. Koran—Surat al-Muminun (v. 97).

The Seventh Legend

The Benevolent Serpent

In the Name of God, the Compassionate, the Merciful. Listen now, Oh well-beloved, to the quaint but true tale which I shall tell concerning this ancient House of the Kretlis which belonged to my Family, and in which I was born and my fathers before me.

Every ancient house, and this one even more than most, has strange legends attached to it which, though of the past, are yet kept in mind from generation to generation.

This tale tells of a snake, a benevolent serpent, that inhabits the place and has always done so, for such serpents dwell only in those houses that are especially favoured, as this one is, by God's blessing, be it here in Cairo or out there among the fourteen Mudiriyas of Egypt. Such snakes are guardians that keep the place in their care, allowing no other reptile to enter, nor evil to harbour within its walls, so that those who live here need have no fear of jinn or *afreet* and may sleep, if they will, with their doors left unlocked.

Now, though this benevolent serpent comes not forth save at night or in secret and is therefore seldom observed, its young, in their folly, may sometimes adventure, as you will learn from what I am about to tell you.

Once, long ago, there lived here in the Bait al-Kretliya my forbear, a devout and pious good man, the Hagg Mohammed, whose children, two little boys, playing together one day here in the court-yard, spied two of the young of our benevolent serpent as they ventured out of their hiding. Thereupon these little boys greatly delighted, pounced on the small snakes, each seizing one and, having tied a string round its belly, took it for his own as a plaything, matching the one against the other, unaware in their innocence of the harm that they did or the danger

Translation of the inscriptions: "This is the story of the owners of the Bait al-Kretliya and their two sons, and of what happened to them on account of the snake because of its young in the Bait al-Kretliya near the Mosque of Ahmad Ibn Tulun. Drawn by Abd al-Aziz Abdu for His Excellency Gayer-Anderson Bey."

they ran. Anon the good parent snake, coming back to her lair from whence she had issued, found her little ones gone and, in much agitation, she hastened to search for them, peering this way and that till very soon she perceived what had happened and that her young ones were now in the hands of their captors, the two little boys of the house. At that, swollen with rage and blind to all else save revenge, she sought out the cupboard where the drinking water is stored in a great *zeer* (earthen-ware vessel),[1] and into this jar she spat out her venom and so poisoned the water that anyone drinking thereof must surely die.

Hardly had she done this than that good pious man, my forbear the Hagg Mohammed, who had been out about some business, returned and, seeing his sons playing each with a little serpent tied by a string round its belly, was greatly alarmed and cried out: 'What in God's name are you doing, O wicked ones? Shame on you! Do you not know you have each made captive a little one of our patron, our protector, our benevolent serpent, without whose blessing the house would surely be desolate? In the name of the Prophet, release your victims at once ere great harm befall you and all of us.'

Thereupon each of those children hung his head much ashamed and affrighted and, hastily obeying his father, freed the young reptile he had made captive, which then wriggled off to his cranny none the worse for the adventure.

Now when the good parent-snake, that benevolent serpent who all this time had been lurking nearby, overheard what this pious man said and observed how, in obedience, his little sons had at once released her offspring uninjured, and when she realized that neither the Sheikh nor his sons meant any harm, her anger subsided forthwith and, full of remorse for what she had done to poison their drinking water, she was greatly concerned how to avert the evil that threatened. And anon her anxiety was greatly increased for she heard the master call out to a serving-maid, 'Go, Aisha, fetch me a cup of cold water from the *zeer*,' it then being the heat of the summer.

Filled now with immediate alarm on behalf of my pious forbear the Hagg Mohammed, that benevolent serpent knew not which way to turn nor what best to do till, by the grace of God, she was prompted so that, hastening off once again to the cupboard where the water was kept, she wound herself round the great *zeer* that was full of it and drew herself tighter and tighter about the vessel till at last it broke and fell asunder with much splash and clatter.

Into nine and ninety pieces was that water jar splintered[2]—for my forbear the Hagg Mohammed counted them one and all afterwards—and the water gushed out and was spilt harmlessly on the floor so that no ill to any came of it.

Then off glided that benevolent serpent back to her hiding place, well pleased at having contrived to avert so great a catastrophe, while the serving-maid who had come at that very moment to the *zeer*-cupboard to fetch her master the drink he had called for, hearing the clatter and seeing the water spilt out and flowing away without a cause, so it seemed to her, ran off herself with a cry of alarm to tell everyone what had happened; and she was greatly afraid, as indeed who would not have been? For she though an afreet or jinn to be the cause of so strange an occurrence.[3]

Notes

1. Every ancient Cairo house, before water was laid on, had a special *zeer*-cupboard (*meziara*), usually at the foot of the stairs, which had *mashrabiya* doors and sides so as to allow a cooling current of air to circulate through and about it. In this cupboard the drinking water was kept (generally under lock and key as a safeguard against poisoning or pollution) in one or more large *zeers*, great egg-shaped jars of porous earthenware through which cooling evaporation can take place.

2. The ninety-nine fragments have, of course, a religious and mythical significance, for the number corresponds to the nine-and-ninety appellations or attributes of Allah, by whose saving grace this miracle had come to pass.

3. Good and evil spirits—jinn, *afreet*, *mareed*, and ghoul—each with its special characteristics, are liable to haunt old houses, dark cupboards and corners, public and private baths, and pestiferous places such as latrines and the like, as well as localities where strange and tragic happenings have occurred which have left an evil vibration behind them. These spirits play an important, almost omnipresent, part in the daily life of the people and therefore take a prominent place in their tales and folklore.

The Eighth Legend

The Enamoured Well[1]

In the Name of God, the Compassionate, the Merciful. Now, Oh my brother, I shall tell you a tale of love with which the magic Well of the Bats has much to do. Know then that once upon a time, long ago, there lived here in the Bait al-Kretliya a rich, widowed lady with her daughter Lutfia, a maiden as fair as a full moon and simple and sweet as a flower.

At the same time there dwelt in a house over the way a handsome youth called Ameen, like Lutfia the only child of his mother, who was also a widow.

Now, much to his parent's regret, this young man showed no desire to marry, being yet scarce acquainted with love and cautious by nature. Indeed the poor woman was nearly distracted, going hither and thither to this one and to that among friends and relations in search of a bride for her son,[2] but all to no purpose, for of whomsoever she spoke, and in no matter what glowing terms, he would answer: 'That's all very well, Oh my Mother, but why should I marry, who have not yet seen the world, or how can I choose, who have never set eyes on a wench I would desire to wed!'

'Then,' cried his mother with some irritation, 'you'll miss all the best girls in Egypt and end up in the arms of a widow. Well, well, so be it. From now on I'll leave you alone to your foolishness and say no more in favour of any, not e'en of Lutfia in the House of the Cretan Lady over the way, though she be the sweetest and most lovely maid of all. Why waste my breath when she too is as loath to marry as you are: but verily, were she willing, you would let her slip through your fingers like a fish back into the sea.'

Now all this she said with a cunning intent to rouse the youth's interest and indeed she succeeded for, left to himself, a great curiosity seized on his

---

Translation of the inscriptions: "The Bait al-Kretliya near Ibn Tulun Cairo. Drawn by Abd al-Aziz Abdu for his Excellency the Miralai Gayer-Anderson Bey."

67

mind so that he fell to wondering why such a girl should be unwilling to marry, and conjuring up a vision so fair that ere long he was deeply in love with his fancy of her whom he had never beheld.

Love is indeed a vexing complaint, for now that young man ceased both to eat and to sleep, while from time to time sighs rent his breast, and he who had scarce ever heeded a maid in the past found himself gazing out through the *mashrabiya* at the house over the way, caring for nought save to catch a glimpse of the loved one.

All day he would sit thus, watching and waiting, but no door opened, nor even a window though indeed, unknown to him, Lutfia, even as he, was all the while peeping through a chink in the hope that she might spy young Ameen for, having heard how handsome he was and yet how averse to be wed, her interest was roused until she too found herself deeply in love with her vision of him just as he was with his fancy of her. Thus sat they, sighing these two, each unbeknown to the other.

'Up with you, lazy one!' cried the girl's mother one day, 'Go draw me a pitcher of water from the well.' Lutfia, after some hesitation, arose and, pulling a shawl that was by her over her head, ran, pail in hand, to do her parent's behest. Across the court-yard she ran to the well in the corner, the Well of the Bats, that magic well of which I have told how,[3] in the days of old Noah when the Ark was stranded here, the last waters of the Flood subsided into its depths, endowing them with miraculous and amorous powers.

Now Lutfia had heard those legends and, for that reason, had always been frightened of the well so that she could scarce bring herself to look down into it, half hoping as she did, yet half fearing to see, as many had told her she might, her lover's reflection therein. On this occasion, though frightened as ever, she none the less could not resist hastily looking down into the well-shaft, for she hoped to see Ameen gazing up at her. But no such sight met her eyes, for as she looked down, lo and behold! those waters that reflected her own face awoke and were agitated because of the beauty cast upon them and, becoming enamoured of her loveliness, they rose and swelled up till they filled the whole shaft of the well to the very top and then they flowed over.[4] Now indeed was Lutfia alarmed, as well she might be, for the waters began to embrace her feet! With a cry, she turned to escape and, as she ran, her shawl fell from her head on to her shoulder.[5] Across the court she ran, out into the street, calling for help. 'Help, help!' cried Lutfia while down-hill she sped, the amorous waves from the well rushing after her in eager pursuit!

Now it happened that on that same day Ameen sat gazing, as had become his wont, out through the lattice of a window. All of a sudden he saw the great eastern door of the Bait al-Kretliya thrown open, and out ran a maiden, frightened and unveiled, so that her incredible beauty filled his eyes; and he saw how the waves kissed her feet as she ran. But, on account of the girl's shawl, he took her to be not Lutfia, but a serving maid. Alarmed, and unable to aid the frightened girl from where he was stationed, Ameen called down to his mother who, perceiving the danger just in time, reached out and, in an instant, caught the girl to her and dragged her in through the door which she quickly closed after her so that the water rushed past it blindly and left the maid unharmed.

On rushed these waters, mad with desire, tumbling over and over till they came to the foot of the hill and were lost in the Khalig,[6] the ancient canal that flowed through Cairo in those days.

(Be it known, Oh my friend, that all this happened by magic, and ever since then the street down which those amorous waters ran in pursuit of that girl has been called, from the source whence they came, 'The Way to the Well of the Bats' as you may see written up to this very day).

Now, the waters having been thus thwarted, Ameen was greatly moved, with joy at the sight of this lovely maiden, and with relief at her safety. His heart stood still; he trembled all over; and now, for the first time in his life, he was really and truly in love with a maiden of flesh and blood, rather than with a mere fantasy; moreover, this serving-maid, as he thought her to be, surpassed all the dreams and desires he had woven about his image of Lutfia. On the instant his mind was made up. 'Oh my Mother,' he called out as he came running down to her, 'I have at last chosen my bride.' 'Have you indeed?' answered that worthy woman, feigning surprise. 'And who might she be, may I ask? Is it Fatima or Hawa, Aisha or Hanim?' 'Oh no, Mother, she is not one of those. She is none other than this serving-maid whom you now hold in your arms!' cried the infatuated youth.

Hearing this, his parent was delighted, for she knew that her greatest desire had come to fulfilment through this miracle of the waters. 'But,' she answered, 'are you so sure that the girl will have *you*, Oh conceited one, for be it known to you that this is no serving-wench as you fancy, but a pasha's daughter, Lutfia, who is, as I told you, the fairest and best of all the girls in Egypt; and be it known to you further-more that she is as loath to be wed as till now thou wert thyself.' 'So she is Lutfia and no serving-maid! Oh Mother, hasten to ask her and gain her consent here and now, else I die of suspense,' cried the lovesick young man.

But it was quite clear that there was no need to ask such a question, for Lutfia had soon perceived how matters stood and that this was Ameen, the very youth she had longed for, and that he was even more handsome than she had pictured him. The maid was too modest, too overcome by emotion, to utter a word but she heaved so deep a sigh and gave such a languishing look that there could be no doubt at all of her consent had the question been asked.

Notes

1. This story, as I have now arranged it, combines several versions which I collected from the Sheikh and others, each differing in minor details from the other. The present text is the one which I broadcast from Cairo on the occasion of King Farouk's marriage in 1938.

2. In olden days, match-making occupied much time and thought in the *hareem*; a professional *dalala* (intermediary) was usually employed and many visits exchanged, without the contracting couple seeing each other till the day of the wedding, though in the

meanwhile they had heard glowing—and often much exaggerated—accounts of each other's charms and attainments.

3. There are other strange stories concerning this well, some of which will be told in the following Legends. It is also mentioned in the fabulous tales of Seif Ibn Yazan (16th century), a series after the manner of *The Arabian Nights*.

4. Sheikh Sulaiman al-Kretli assured me that his grandfather, a devout and careful man, would on no account let his young daughters or good-looking slave-girls draw water from this well for fear of similar consequences.

5. The loss of this head-covering, a shawl commonly worn by the more humble girls and young children instead of the veil or yashmak, not only revealed the girl's beauty but also, as appears later, caused Ameen to suppose that she was merely a serving-maid.

6. This ancient canal (the Khalig), dating from Pharaonic days, that traversed Cairo from North to South, was filled-in during the cholera epidemic of 1896 for reasons of hygiene and converted into a tramway. Many gardens and palaces, as well as much mediaeval history, clustered round the Khalig; the annual 'opening of the mouth' of this canal at High Nile is still an interesting ceremony, though now shorn of its former magnificence.

The Ninth Legend

Sultan al-Watawit
and His Seven Daughters

سُلطانُ الوَطاوِيطُ وبناتهِ السَبع

In the Name of God, the Compassionate, the Merciful. Now, Oh my honoured friend, let us return to the Well, 'The Well of the Bats,' about whose magical and amorous waters I have already spoken.

This ancient Well under the arch in a corner of our court, now little used and little considered, was once famous far and wide. So much was this the case that, as I have already recounted, the road leading uphill to the House and the Mosque is still called 'The Way to the Well of the Bats,' which is still writ up in order to direct all who wish to visit our famous Well; and they were many in the olden days, for its waters have always been known to possess magical and beneficent properties; and that is hardly to be wondered at, since they flowed into this shaft from the Great Flood as it subsided, and left Noah's Ark stranded here on this hill of Yashkur; but of this I have already told you!

Yes, our Well had long been renowned for the many cures it has wrought, lovers it has served, and countless strange happenings concerning it which have taken place here in our midst. But above all, it is renowned as the haunt and home of the Sultan al-Watawit, the King of the Jinn, who inhabits a palace within it with his seven fair daughters amidst vast treasures which are guarded by his magic.

This explains why, at the Sultan's demand, the Bait al-Kretliya was built round the magic well by my forbears, instead of a shaft being sunk in the midst of the house as was the usual procedure. There were also various secret reasons which caused the Sultan to remain for long in league with my kin, to whom he gave much gold as a reward, and this they stored away in a chamber under the floor of the *hareem*, a procedure that resulted in a catastrophe to my Family to which I have already

---

Translation of the inscriptions: "The Well of the Bats is in the Court of the Bait al-Kretliya. At the bottom of this well there is a beautiful palace inhabited by the Sultan al-Watawit, together with his seven sons [sic]. Surrounded by a large treasure." Note: On this plate the artist has written "Sons" in error; it should be "Daughters."

referred and of which I shall tell more in due course.

The Sultan is still in his palace and his seven fair daughters lie around him under a spell,[1] each in her golden bed; and all so fast asleep that if any intrude and arouse them they hardly stir, but murmur, 'Take all you will and leave us to our slumbers.' Their father guards them—and his palace and treasure—by his sorceries, changing himself at times into a bat, a shape he assumes at will, in which guise he may sometimes be seen of an evening to enter or leave the mouth of the well. All that closely guarded treasure remains still for the finding, but it is by no means easy to come by, for very many have tried but so far no one has succeeded.

I have tried myself—on more than one occasion when I was a young man—and always I used *mandal* (divination),[2] but even that method failed though, as a rule, I am successful with it.

Some of those who have set out on that venture have never returned, but were either lost in perdition or chose to bide where they found themselves. And, strange though it may sound, the good King of the Jinn sometimes helps the wives or the widows of those who have not returned from the venture of seeking to rob him, should they be needy, and he does it in the following manner. He sees to it that, now and again, when such a one lowers her bucket into the well, a coin of gold or of silver is dropped into it for her to recover. I knew one poor woman who was thus supported for years and once I, myself when I lowered a bucket, felt the rope nearly jerked from my hands by some unseen power, and as I pulled up the vessel it came spinning so that half the

water was spilt; but there, sure enough, in the midst of the pail was a bright piece of gold.

Though, as I say, no one so far has come by this treasure, it is well known through the writings in magical books how best to obtain it. First of all, well provided with rope, rations, a lantern, and all else that such a venture may need, and not forgetting to recite the *Fatha* and to commend yourself to God's care, you are lowered, as once I was, on the end of a rope to where the shaft opens out at the water's level into a chamber.[3] From the east and west of this space issue two hidden passages, and at the entrance stands an *afreet* who works a *shadoof*,[4] lifting water out of the well and pouring it down these two inclined ways, one of which leads to the palace of the Sultan and the treasure, the other to an unknown bottomless pit of destruction.

Now which is which of these two passages no one can tell, save by divination, divine intuition, or by some sorcerer's spell. Yet on the choice of direction depends whether the seeker shall survive and emerge a rich man by God's grace, or fall and disappear entirely, never again to be seen or heard of: for so steep are the two paths, and so slippery, that once started on either one cannot stop.

Before setting out on this adventure one must also learn, through sorcery or *mandal*, not only which way to turn at the well's end but also the magical word that shall open the door of the Palace if one gets there, for it is locked and sealed with Solomon's seal.[5]

As for myself, on one of the occasions long ago when I attempted this undertaking and hoped to succeed in it, I made all ready but my *mandal* failed me;

so I had recourse to an old Sudanese woman, a sorceress, and I was about to have the secrets revealed to me by *zar* (sorcery),[6] but the spirit she summoned to our assistance persisted in demanding the sacrifice of an Abyssinian slave-girl, and so I had reluctantly to abandon the project at the last moment. That is why you see me now a poor man and, moreover, unable to tell you more concerning that rich treasure, but let me be thankful that I am still alive in the midst of the living; 'the praise be to God,' for might I not be falling for ever and ever. 'The Lord pours upon us steadfastness and sets our feet firm.'[7]

Notes

1. In another version of this story it is seven *sons*, not daughters, of the Sultan who were so bewitched; and it will be seen that in his illustration to this Legend, Abd al-Aziz calls them 'sons.' In either case, the idea must have been derived from 'The Seven Sleepers' and their dog, given such prominence in the Koran.

   In that tale, just as 'his little dog' went with Tobias and the angel, so the little dog, 'al-Rakim,' accompanied the seven pre-Moslem youths who hid from religious persecution in a cave and were there spelled to sleep. The self-confident hound wagged its tail and spake, saying: 'Go to sleep and I will guard you.' But in spite of that he, too, finally dozed off; none the less he was eventually admitted to Heaven with his seven masters, the only dog as far as I know to be so honoured.

   It is interesting to note in this connection that a recent *Fatwa*, issued in April 1940 by the Sheikh of al-Azhar, places dogs in as privileged a position as they hold amongst ourselves, although they have for centuries been considered unclean, almost untouchable creatures in Islam.

2. Divination (*mandal*) through the offices of a virgin-boy—one who has not yet arrived at puberty, who has never been burnt by fire or cut this hand with a knife, or been bitten by a dog (in the Sudan it is sometimes added that he must never have been stung by a scorpion)—is a usual resource, especially in the location of treasure, the detection of theft, or the recovery of lost objects. The lad gazes into a bowl of oil or water, or a pool of ink in a spoon, or in the cupped palm of his hand and, in a state of semi-trance, answers questions put to him as to what he sees. His words and visions are interpreted by an experienced diviner such as Sheikh Sulaiman.

3. This is a fact for, though I have not gone down it, I have explored the well as far as possible with a lantern and plumb-line. From a narrow round shaft it expands into an eight foot square chamber and this is undercut in all directions, just above water-level, into a wider space of unknown dimensions. The well is nearly forty feet in depth, cut through solid rock, and at mid-Nile contains about ten feet of crystal-clear, slightly brackish water, somewhat purgative in quality, which may account for its medicinal renown in days past.

4. No other country has such an ancient, primitive, and yet ingenious variety of irrigation devices as Egypt, a country that depends on lifted water to a degree unknown elsewhere.

   The *shadoof* (in Upper Egypt the *ud*) consists of a goat-skin bucket at the end of a long pole which is pivoted to an upright and provided with a counter lever (a large ball of dried clay). This pole is manipulated by one man and is the most ancient and unchanged of all water-lifting devices: one sees it depicted in a tomb painting at Thebes (1500 B.C.) and doubtless it harks back to the very beginning of Egyptian civilization.

5. This consists of two equilateral triangles superimposed and centred so as to form a six-pointed star. The sign has its place in Free Masonry and in nearly every Moslem and Hebrew magical formula, because, as in the case of Solomon's own ring, the *Ism al-Azim* (the one unknown of the hundred names of God) was engraved in its centre.

6. *Zar* (sorcery or magic) is believed in by most Mohammedans and is studied and practised by many of the more conservative or old-fashioned. Though condemned by the Koran, the Prophet countenanced it in the Traditions provided it is 'good' magic, for there are two kinds. The first is Divine, or 'good', magic, a sublime and legitimate science allied to astrology, and centred in the Ism al-Azim, and associated with the Prophet's ninety-nine known names or attributes. It is abetted by all good spirits. The second kind of magic is Satanic, 'bad,' or 'black' magic, which depends on the agency of the devil and the active Collaboration of all evil spirits. Between these two varieties exists a popular middle course, a mixture of both. To this category the magic herein described would seem to have conformed.

7. Koran—Surat al-Baqara.

The Tenth Legend

More Magic of the Well of the Bats

In the Name of God, the Compassionate, the Merciful. Today, Oh beloved friend, I shall relate two very short tales, but in a special way, for I shall chant them to you; they might perhaps the better be termed spells or traditions. They are in rhyme since ancient times but nowhere writ down, being passed on by word of mouth from generation to generation. They both concern the Well of the Bats, about which I have already told you two tales.

The first of the rhymes which I shall chant to you tells how a young virgin lover (either girl or boy) who comes hither and gazes down into the depths of the well on a moonlight night may see what shall be seen. For so it is set down in this 'Rhyme of Love Magic':[1]

If thou be maiden without stain,
Or lad till now unversed in love,
That yet no knife has cut or fire burnt,

Nor dog has bit, then[2] not in vain
To this old well-head turn and look within,
And down a little pebble throw;
At the night's noon, that milk-white hour
When the moon full-grown,
Doth ride through heaven like a houri fair
In her full loveliness.
And when the troubled circles cease
If in that mirror thou shalt see
The face of one look up to thee
As thou at it look'st down,
Then know for sure thy true love's face,
This magic well reveals to thee.

Now listen to the second rhyme of the magic well which I shall chant to you. It is even briefer than the first, but more serious, for it concerns the Word of God recited by angel-voices. Nor is this manifestation

---

Translation of the inscriptions: "If a virgin girl or a virgin boy, who has not been bitten by a dog, burnt by fire or had his hand cut by a knife, looks into the waters of the Well of the Bats in the court of the Bait al-Kretliya at night by full moonlight he will, by the grace of God, see the face of his lover."

any less true than the first, for I am acquainted with several who, having performed the religious ablution[3] and approached this well with a clean heart and God's blessing while the moon was at the full and from its height shining straight down the shaft on to the waters below, have heard what is to be heard as here set forth in this 'Rhyme of the Echoed Word':

> Ye pure of heart and spiritually clean
> Now when the moon shines full and clear
> Approach this ancient well and lean
> Over it listening. Ye shall hear
> God's echoed word by angels sung

> Float up to you in cadence fair,
> Like pearls of blessing deftly strung
> On unseen filaments of air.

Surely it is such strange and beautiful happenings, as set forth in those two rhymes, that prove the constant presence of God in our midst: for is it not written in the Blessed Book: 'Among his signs are the night and the day, the sun and the moon' and again it is written: 'Three persons speak not together but He is a fourth, nor five but He is a sixth, and be they few or many, wherever they may be He is with them.'[4] The praise be to God.[5]

Notes

1. I have ventured to paraphrase the two short rhymes and put them into verse.

2. The qualifications required of the boy must necessarily exclude many, if not most, lads and, one cannot help suspecting, supply the needful excuse should the venture fail. Much the same essentials are demanded, as we have already seen (the Ninth Legend, Note 4), of a youth used for purposes of divination (*mandal*).

3. Religious ablution (*wudu*) is required before saying the appointed Moslem prayers and, though it only involves washing the face, hands, arms (as high as the elbows), feet, and ankles, the ritual is complex, as can be observed in Egypt at dawn or in the evening before sunset beside river or canal. In the desert, where water is not procurable, it is permitted to use sand as a substitute.

4. These two quotations from the Koran are Surat Fussilat (V. 37) and Surat Mujadala (V. 7).

5. I would like to draw special attention to the skill and imagination displayed in the accompanying illustration by Abd al-Aziz. In the first place, it will be observed that the faces reflected in the water are transposed so that the boy looking down sees the reflection of the girl's face instead of his own, and *vice versa*. The full moon illumines the entire scene, both above and below ground level, with a pleasantly eerie effect which is enhanced by the presence of the bat representing Sultan al-Watawit, and by numerous night-birds.

   A further air of 'magic casements,' as well as an echo of the other mystic qualities of the place and a reminder of evil lurking amidst the good, are indicated to the right by the enamoured water's pursuit of Lutfia (as told in our Eighth Legend), and to the left by the blind thief leaving the house (as recounted in the Thirteenth Legend). The motives of the mosque, house, and tomb and the tree blazon (extreme right) are all re-echoed here.

The Eleventh Legend

The Secret Chamber[1]

In the Name of God, the Compassionate, the Merciful. Give ear, Oh honoured friend, to the tale of a man's avarice and the folly of women and how these led to a sad ending.

If you will look in the north-east corner of the *hareem* on the first floor of this house, a corner that is suspended, as it were, on an arch immediately over our magical well in the depths of which, as you know, dwells the King of the Jinn in his palace surrounded by fabulous treasure; if you look, as I say, in that corner, you will find there under the matting a loose flagstone with an iron ring through its centre and, raising this, you will discover a small wooden trap-door through which, having looked and perceived the place empty, you may, if you wish, descend into a chamber beneath, which has no light and but little air.

Know then that this little closet is called the *makh-ba*, or hiding place, for it is here that things of value—money and jewels and suchlike—were kept and in it, too, a person might hide for a short time and no one be the wiser.

When the French came to Egypt under their Sultan Bonaparte, my great-grandfather, a prudent and careful man, hid many things of value here and sent all his women away in a boat to the South. My grandmamma, who was a child at the time, remembered this clearly and told me as a boy how she brought her doll to the *makhba* and insisted on its being hid there along with the family treasure until she should come back and take it again in her arms, as in fact she did.

Suchlike and many other interesting tales could be told without doubt of this place, but the most strange of all is the one I shall now tell you, which concerns the Well of the Bats, also over which this chamber is

---

Translation of the inscriptions: "Under the floor of the *hareem* of the Bait al-Kretliya there is a secret room which, so it is alleged, was once filled with gold-dust from the treasure of the Sultan al-Watawit: but the ignorant Ladies who found it threw it out of the house thinking it was chaff. Moreover, on the roof of the *hareem*, there was once a fortress which fired its cannon-balls on to the Citadel of the great Mohammed Ali Pasha until the Pasha discovered it."

poised, and to which some say it is joined by a passage, though in the darkness none has yet found the way.[2] And now I will tell you my tale in God's name.

In the Koran it is written: 'We have given him such treasure that its keys would burden a whole company of strong men.'[3] So it was with my kinsman who lived here long since and was given such wealth that, had it not been for the folly of women, much gold might still remain here in our keeping and I be a rich man, a Pasha perhaps, instead of as you now see me, a poor Sheikh who stands at the door of the rich. But there! We all stand at God's door and wait on His will, so in the end all things are equal and for the best.

That forbear of mine was a Turk, the Agha Saleem al-Kretli Bek (Turkish for 'Bey'), who, though a pious man, was avaricious to such a degree that he thought, schemed, and dreamed of nothing but gold. Yes, of gold alone, not of what gold would buy, for he purchased not land or houses with all his great wealth, nor trinkets for his women, nor aught for himself save the bare necessities of life.

Though so rich and of high station, a Bey, he went about in worn clothes[4] and rode a lean ass, with no one to run at his side or carry his sword or his *shibbuk* (long tobacco pipe),[5] he who could well have afforded a horse and syce, or two into the bargain. So mean, such a miser was he that to his women he gave scarce enough cloth to cover them decently, and to his servants, as to himself, barely the food and the drink they required to keep them still breathing so that they say, his cupboards being empty, even the rats quit the place.

Now this man, who left no means untried to scrape and save and gather in money, had made a pact with the Sultan al-Watawit of whom I have spoken and who dwelt, and yet dwells, in the Well of the Bats. The pact concerned some secret matter of great import, and for his help in the affair the Sultan paid him vast sums which, at regular intervals, he drew up in a bucket in the form of gold-dust from the bottom of the well.

This dust the Bey would carry by stealth up the women's stairs to the *hareem* above and, pulling up the stone slab in the floor, would cast it into the *makhba*.

This he did thinking such a place the most fit and safest in the house and, indeed, so it was, for here only the women can enter and no man may come. Moreover, women, though prying, are not clever in these matters and can easily be deceived. Therefore when any one of them questioned him, saying, 'Oh my master, what do you there in the *makhba*?' or 'What is that you throw into the darkness?' he would answer benignly, 'Nothing, Oh sweetheart, nothing of value, it's only *tibn*, chaff for the donkey to eat, for the bins are full in the stable below,' adding reprovingly, 'So now be off to your work and leave me to mine as God wills.' Soon his women were satisfied and paid no more heed to what he did at the *makhba*.

All things went well for the Bey, and the secret chamber was nigh filled with the yellow dust when, alas! He took to him a new wife on whom he doted. A comely young person she was, but a busybody who would put all things in their order and everyone right in a trice. One day, while her husband was away on a journey, this young woman chanced to open the *makhba* and look within. 'What's all this litter that fills our *makhba*?' she called out to a serving-maid. 'Oh, that's only *tibn*, my mistress,' answered the wench. 'Just chaff for the donkey to eat which our master throws in there because the bins in the stable are full.' 'Chaff for the donkey. I like that! Does he take us all for she-asses? Well then we'll eat his *tibn*! Come, cast it all out of the window forthwith!'

'I hear and obey, so be it,' answered the girl and, fetching another to help her, they cleared the place, after considerable labour, with a shovel and basket. At last not one speck remained in the *makhba*, for they had thrown all that good gold-dust out of the window into the street below where it was swept away or trod under foot and lost for ever and ever.

So it is that those things we set our hearts upon turn to ashes, and so it was with him whose heart was set on such dross above all else. Now the Master, when he returned from his journey, went at once to the *hareem*, wishing to lift the stone and rejoice his eyes with the sight of all that gold-dust in the secret chamber. And there, his young wife, feeling some apprehension at what she had done, ran to him with open arms, crying, 'Oh my Lord, I've tidied up everything in there. After all, we are not she-asses who desire a pile of *tibn* and old chaff to be stored in our stable! I have had it all thrown out of the window and the *makhba* made ready for its proper uses!'

'You've thrown what from the window?' cried that horror-stricken man. 'Your worthless old *tibn*,' answered his wife. 'My precious *tibn*, you mean!' echoed the miser. 'My golden *tibn*! My gold!' he cried; and those were the last words he ever spoke, for there on the spot he was struck dumb! Some say it was by the Sultan al-Watawit, lest his secret be given away. Be that as it may, the power of his limbs also forsook him, so that he could but lie abed without speech and helpless, else it would have fared ill with his busy young wife.

The Agha Saleem Bek al-Kretli never recovered. He withered away and soon afterwards died and was buried, unable to sustain that grievous blow which had deprived him of what he loved most on this earth. Such was the judgment of God. 'May Allah the Compassionate, the Merciful, pity him on the day of his reckoning.'

They say, too, that the King of the Jinn, in his anger at the waste of all that good gold, smote also the young wife, widowed now, with a lingering illness from which she, too, never recovered. Ever since then, even up to our own times, in order to propitiate him and obtain his good offices, women in these parts are accustomed to cast offerings to the jinn through the trap-door into that *makhba*, now empty, which once was brim-full of pure gold.[7]

Notes

1. Every ancient house of any pretension in Old Cairo had one or more *makhba* (secret chamber). These are of two kinds, the one a chamber under the floor with little or no ventilation, the other a small, concealed living-room above floor level. The Bait al-Kretliya has two of the former (about one of which this story is told) and one of the latter variety. The under-floor chambers are designed primarily to hide away

objects of value. They are entered by raising a loose flagstone (ordinarily concealed under matting and rugs). The secret chamber in our *hareem* is admirably shown in the illustration, both in its relation to the well-head below and the *hareem* above, with its windows beyond opening on to the street. This *makhba* is eleven feet long, four broad, and nearly four in height, so that its capacity is considerable.

The second, more unusual, type of secret chamber (*audat as-sirr*)—one example of which is to be found in the Bait al-Kretliya—takes the form of a small, unsuspected living-room or rooms with air and light admitted; it is entered through a concealed door usually made to resemble a wall-cupboard, or one section of it, as is the case in our example.

Besides secret closets and chambers, there are also in all old Arab houses, particularly in their *hareem* apartments, what one may call cubby-holes behind movable panels or in the masonry above cupboards, which admit the hand to a space perhaps a foot square. The Bait al-Kretliya has at least half a dozen such, three of them in the *hareem*.

2. Our secret chamber is indeed situated exactly above the well-shaft (as is shown in the illustration) and this fact, coupled with the magic reputation of the waters below, doubtless gave rise to the belief that the two were connected.

3. Koran—Surat al-Qasas (V. 76).

4. As a matter of fact the Bey was in no way unusual in this respect for, during Mameluke days of violence and disorder, it was as much as a man's life, certainly his fortune, was worth to display outward and visible signs of wealth and well-being.

5. The Turkish *shibbuk*, in contrast with the *shisha* (hubble-bubble), was a pipe with a straight stem five to six feet long made, as a rule, of cherry wood or jessamine; at one end was a small bowl of clay, china, brass, or stone and at the other an elaborate jewelled and enamelled amber or glass mouthpiece six to eight inches long, often very beautiful and costly. Sixty years ago these pipes were universally used and accompanied their owners, carried by a syce or servants, wherever they went: now they have entirely disappeared, perhaps because their length proved too unwieldy in these crowded and hurried times.

6. In the days before drinking water was laid on, it had to be brought from the Nile, since Cairo wells are all slightly brackish and canal and pond water is foul: such a valued commodity was it, that the daily amount of drinking water—as well as of food and wages—was often stipulated in contracts of employment.

7. This is borne out by what the Author found when he first came to the House. On opening up the *makhba* it was found to be half filled with debris, a large part of which consisted of little dried-up offertory bunches of flowers (reminiscent of those from the tomb of Tutankhamen), as well as various scraps of cloth, doubtless from personal clothing, such as one sees tied to the nail-studded door of the Bab Zuweila, in token of vows fulfilled or undertaken, or of favours sought.

The Twelfth Legend

A Saint on the Premises[1]

In the Name of God, the Compassionate, the Merciful. And now, Oh honoured friend, let me tell you the tale of our Saint on the premises, the beneficent Haroon al-Huseini, son of the Prophet's grandson, the martyr Husein, who was slain at Kerbela and whose blessed head still rests in our midst.

During the reign of the Fatimites, when that blessed head was brought here to Cairo and placed where it now lies in the mosque of Hassaneyn by the Khan al-Khalili, there came with this holy relic the remains of many more of our Lord Mohammed's own blood, God bless and preserve them; and amongst these, the body of our own Master Haroon, son of Ali and Fatima and therefore the Prophet's great grand-child.

With much state in procession they brought him and buried him here, where a tomb had been made ready to harbour him and where those good people, my forbears who then lived in this house, rejoiced to have in their midst and keep in their care such a cherished and blessed relic.

Having lowered their burden into its tomb-chamber under the earth, and there set it out in pure sand on a shelf and covered it over with a white burial sheet, and sprinkled cut flowers and herbs thereon, they left the Saint here, his face turned towards Mecca, and here he has lain ever since bringing peace to the place.

All this I know, having lived most of my life in his domed tomb; and once, as a young man, I descended into the chamber beneath at the bidding of Sidi Haroon himself. This I undertook with two others, both pious men, who waited above while I, opening the trap-door, let down a ladder and descended into the tomb chamber: there I saw what I shall now describe to you, for though I took no lantern with me

---

Translation of the inscriptions: "In the days of the Fatimites the body of our Master Haroon, the son of our Master al-Huseini, the son of the daughter of the Prophet, was brought here and buried under the dome which is in the garden of the Bait al-Kretliya; thereafter its presence illumined the darkness. Drawn by Abd al-Aziz Abdu." On the canopy of the bier "The bier of Haroon." On the books "Allah," "There is no God but God," etc.

I beheld none the less everything clearly, for the place was filled with a sweet smell and a rare effulgence of light that proceeded from the Saint's body; and though I dared not lift up the sheet that covered his face and look under it, I set my hands gently on his corpse and felt it there, perfect in shape and in no way destroyed, for so it is with the remains of the blessed.[2]

I can remember, too, as a young man, a similar happening when, in the course of some repairs to the tomb-mosque of al-Ghuri—the Mameluke Sultan who had been killed in battle near Aleppo at the age of seventy in the year 997 hegira (A.D. 1615)—I was deputed to enter the burial chamber and, when they raised the stone which sealed the mouth of the tomb, I descended into the vault accompanied by the *hanooti* (corpse-washer) and we beheld—and on this occasion we had a strong lamp with us—the body of the Sultan lying there wrapped in his burial sheet on pure sand.

How many and great the blessings that come from the presence of Sidi Haroon in our midst it is hard to assess, for the ways of the righteous are hid and all is not revealed, save unto God: none the less let me relate to you some of those blessings about which I know. For example, many years since, I was in a house on fire when the floor I stood upon fell through and I found myself, as it were, in a furnace with no one to save me, for it was as though I stood in the very midst of Gehenna,[3] with no way of escape. Then I thought myself lost, but lo! Sidi Haroon came walking towards me and, taking my hands, led me forth so that I was saved, while others who were with me perished, destroyed by the flames. For long after that I lay between life and death while the Saint watched over me, saying, 'Fear nothing, Oh

Sulaiman, for you shall live to serve me again.' And so it was that I recovered and though my eyes were burnt out, their sight was restored; and have I not tended him from when I was eight years old until now, when I am eighty and more, even as my fathers served him before me?

During all these years Sidi Haroon has often come to me in his actual shape, sometimes in waking but more often in my dreams, telling me what best to do or what he would have me leave undone.[4] So it was I once met a young man quite close to here who said, 'Tell me, O my uncle, where is the grave of Haroon?' Shocked at his lack of respect, I answered, rebuking him, 'Our master Haroon al-Huseini you mean, peace be upon him,' and I added, 'I go that way myself; come you with me therefore.' And so I led him here to this tomb, whereupon he cried out, 'Know you not who I am? I am he who lies buried beneath, I am Haroon al-Huseini himself, and I would have you observe that my dome is cracked and about to fall in upon thy head, see to it therefore for thine own sake if not for mine!'

At that I looked up in fear and surprise and beheld for the first time that, as he had said, there was a great crack in the dome which seemed like to fall in upon me and I said, 'On my head be it, Oh Master, if I have not this blemish repaired forthwith.' And as I said this I turned my eyes towards him and lo! He was gone and none stood in his place. You may be sure I caused the dome to be repaired without delay!

Once, moreover, the saint appeared to my mother, then a young woman who, at night, seeing a light in the *qa'ah*, peeped in through a chink in the door and beheld there a young man who, with others, conducted a *zikr*[5] and again, though there were no lamps in the room, the place was illumined by light shining from the young man, and he said to her—although she was not in the room with him but without—'Fear not, good woman, I make this rhythmic intercession for the recovery of thy husband who is grievously ill.' Now my mother knew nothing of this, for her husband, my father, was at the time far away on a journey. Yet it proved just as the Saint had said, and my father recovered and came back to tell us how he had been sick unto death until he saw the Saint in a vision as my mother had seen him, and at the same time as she, and from then on he had recovered his strength until he was now stronger than ever before.

Such are a few of the blessings and benefits which our Master Haroon has bestowed upon us here in my time. Of others I shall tell you anon, for of a truth though unseen, his presence is always with us in this house, like a light that illumines our way as it shall thine for the future, Oh honoured friend.

'Verily, God is all-wise and all-knowing Who does as He chooses.'

Notes

1. It is not unusual in old Mameluke houses to find a saint or sheikh buried on the premises; such a relic was, and still is, considered extremely propitious. The remains may be already on the site when a house comes to be built upon it (it would be an almost unheard-of act of impiety to remove them even should one wish to do so) or else the relic may be brought to the spot by the owner.

   In our case, the tomb is situated at the South-East corner of the House, into which it formerly opened through a small door. This door is now walled up and the entry is now direct from the street.

2. There are apparently two schools of thought in the matter. According to one, the saintly body remains intact; according to the other, it crumbles and is refined away to 'nothing' so that only the saint's spiritual presence remains. I have been assured of this on several occasions, once by the keeper of the tomb of Sheikh Seria in the Turkish sixteenth-century mosque of Sulaiman Pasha at the Citadel. I asked the keeper what was inside and he answered, 'The Sheikh is there, but only as a handful of dust. God bless and preserve him.'

3. Gehenna, the place of flames, a nether region reserved for men and jinn; there the evil and unbelieving are consigned to everlasting fire 'unless the Lord shall will it otherwise.' According to the Koran, Abraham was betrayed to the flames by Nimrod but—very much as in our story—the Angel Gabriel came to his aid, and God, decreeing, 'Oh fire, burn thou cold and be to Abraham a safety.' Only the cords that bound him were consumed so that he might escape.

4. One of the traditional sayings of the Prophet is: 'Whoso seeth me in sleep seeth me truly, for Satan cannot assume the similitude of my form.'

5. A *zikr* is a rhythmic repetition of some holy word or phrase, such as 'Oh God,' 'He is One,' or just 'He,' accompanied by swayings of the body and movements of the head and arms, performed by a group of men in unison so that a state of religious intoxication is reached. The tempo gradually increases and many collapse or have to fall out. The whirling and howling Dervish performances now, alas, done away with were but different forms of this ritual.

The Thirteenth Legend

More of Our Saint's Miraculous Benefits

In the Name of God, the Compassionate, the Merciful. I said, Oh my dear friend, that I would tell you more of the miraculous benefits which come to those such as yourself who dwell in this house through the presence, in our midst, of our master Haroon al-Huseini, and of the many miracles he has performed in times past. Most surely he will continue to manifest in the future to the advantage of those here and in this neighbourhood.

Besides those cases which I have already recounted listen, I pray you, to what follows.

On one occasion when my father, may Allah be merciful to him on the day of reckoning, was but a child, a workman fell by ill-chance off the roof from high above the tomb of our Master Haroon, and under other conditions would have been killed for sure, but in this case it was not so for, being a good man, a devout Dervish of the Ahmadiya brethren,[1] he hung, suspended by the breath of our Saint, in mid air and was let down so lightly that not a bone in his body was broken nor any hurt came to him; the praise be to Allah!

Once, too, a young child of the house, playing here in the court, stretched out his hands in his innocence to caress a mad dog that had entered by chance when the Saint's unseen hand caught him up by the hair of his head out of harm's way and set him down elsewhere in safety so that he escaped quite unharmed.[2] Thank God for his mercies!

Yet again, out of necessity a forbear of mine was driven to mortgage and, finally, to sell the Bait al-Kretliya, but behold! when he and the purchaser were about to clasp hands and recite the *Fatha* upon it,[3] thus clinching the bargain, at that

---

Translation of the inscriptions: "In the days of the Lady of the Kretlis, a thief entered the House to steal but, as the House was under the protection of our Master Haroon, the thief was struck blind and lost his sight through the influence of the Saint, and he remained three days and nights lost in the House and could not find his way out until the Lady of the Kretlis discovered him and took pity on him and let him go free. Drawn by Abd al-Aziz." On the squatting figure left, "the Lady owner of the Bait al-Kretliya." On the standing figure, "the thief."

moment he felt something pressed over his mouth that deprived him of speech so that he could not affirm his consent, while at the same time the pen he held in his hand, about to sign away our possession, was snatched from him so that he could not write; and so the transaction was postponed. Next day it transpired that, quite unexpectedly, my kinsman had come into a fortune sufficient to pay off the mortgage and keep him in comfort here for the rest of his life without further need to dispose of this house, and so the sale was not concluded. Allah be praised!

But perhaps the strangest of all such strange happenings has to do with a thief, an evil man who, when I was a boy, entered the house to rob it but was stayed in his wicked intent and requited as Allah willed through our Saint's intervention.

Thus it came about: One day we children, playing on the roof, saw this man as a shadow thrown upon a wall and, in our terror thinking this an *afreet* and fearing to look round and behold it, we ran off screaming to tell our mother. By the time she had reassured us and come back with us to see what was amiss, behold, an ill-looking man was there who groped his way through the daylight, and we perceived at once that this was no ghost but a blind man who could not harm anyone.[4] At that, we children ran towards him and, striking him with our fists and with small sticks which we had in our hands, called out in derision 'Bad man, blind man, what do you here?'

To all this he made no resistance but only threw up his arms and cried with many tears, saying, 'I am indeed a thief and came here to steal but I have been struck blind by some unseen power.' Thereupon my

mother silenced us while she caused food and drink to be brought for the man, who was too weak to say more. After he had drunk and eaten he greatly revived and recounted his story.

He told how he had entered the house unobserved between dusk and dark while the door was unguarded, three days before as he judged it, for he could tell night from day only by the sounds in the house; how, creeping into the *hareem* with intent to lay hands on what jewels he could find, he had hidden there till midnight before venturing forth; how, scarce had he come into the room where the women lay sleeping than a bright light shone forth intensely and, wherever he looked, it was there, burning his eyes till it blinded him; how, in affright, he had then felt his way to the door but since he could no longer see nor judge daylight from darkness, he had lost himself in the house and knew not whither he went; how he had hidden for those three days in chests and in cupboards with nothing to eat or to drink, and by night had groped stealthily about, unable to find either food or his way out of the house, even though empty-handed, so that now he was well-nigh dead from hunger and thirst and weakness.

It was, of course, the protective presence and power of Sidi Haroon that had confused and afflicted him thus, though the Saint himself did not appear.

On hearing all this my mother, a kind and compassionate woman, was moved in her pity to say, 'Oh thief, if our Saint hath seen fit to smite thee thus blind for thy sins, nought then remains for me to do but to pardon thee. Therefore go now and take this coin in thy wallet to meet thy needs and come no more. Adopt some better means of livelihood, I beseech thee, so that God, in return, may restore thee thy sight.' With this benediction she led him to the door of the house and dismissed him.

So it was that he who had come to steal went away empty-handed but for my mother's alms, being thus both rewarded and punished for what he had set out to do but had failed to accomplish, thanks to the good office of Sidi Haroon, by the will and with the assistance of Allah the Protector, the Powerful, the Prevailing, in whose name such things are wrought.

Nor did the thief ever recover his sight, for his life had been evil and this affliction which had thus been laid upon him was just. For long thereafter he dwelt in these parts as a blind beggar who had once been a rich man; for, seeing him helpless, his women and accomplices forsook him and divided up between them all he had amassed by his cunning. Thus he was left penniless, an object of pity and a warning to others; for those of the neighbourhood would point him out to strangers and tell them the tale I have told you. Is it not written: 'They plotted their plots; but even their craftiness was under the control of God.'"[5]

Notes

1. Dervishes, of which there are four main brotherhoods in Egypt, are numerous and still exert an influence in this country despite strenuous and rapidly succeeding efforts of late years both here and in Turkey to stamp them out. Some are men of ascetic life; many are imposters to a greater or lesser degree.

2. Young boys, whose heads are by custom kept close-cropped or shaven, have often a substantial side-lock left—as was the case with the Pharaonic boy-god Horus and young princes and nobles of that day—to act as a convenient handle by which their guardian-angels could snatch them out of harm's way when need be, or by which they could be carried up to heaven. This leaving of a side-lock on little boys' heads as an emergency handle was a prevalent custom in the Sudan and even more so in Arabia before the 1914/18 war.

3. In clinching a bargain, signing a contract (or marriage), etc., or coming to any other agreement of importance, hands are clasped and the *Fatha* (that beautiful opening chapter of the Koran which is the equivalent of, and bears a striking similarity to, the Christian 'Lord's Prayer') is recited in unison by the parties concerned.

4. The thief cannot have been a hardened criminal, for he appears to have been whole, though the Koranic punishment for theft—applied, however, only under certain aggravated circumstances—was, for the first conviction, amputation of the right hand; for the second, of the left foot; for the third, of the left hand; for the fourth, of the right foot—lenient punishments in comparison with the hanging of a boy of seventeen for the theft of a lamb in England as recently as 1860!

5. Koran—Surat Ibraheem (V. 46).

The Fourteenth Legend

Mosque and House
Fall on Evil Days But Rise Again[1]

In the Name of God, the Compassionate, the Merciful. My honoured friend, let me now tell you the sad story of the decline of the great Mosque of Ibn Tulun and of the Bait al-Kretliya, though this story is indeed more part of the history of olden days than a Legend.

Man's brief day is soon over and, when it is past, none recall him nor keep him in memory. His dwelling, deserted, falls into ruin, while all he possessed is dispersed amongst others.[2] Such is God's will! And so it befell that after hundreds of years in occupation of this old house, passing as it did from father to son in prosperous circumstances, at length evil times came. The place was mortgaged and divided in ownership and, from being a spacious abode, was split up and partitioned off into tenements for poor and humble persons to live in and, amongst these, one was occupied by myself and my family,

and we shared but a part of the dwelling that our forbears had inherited and held so long in complete and sole possession; and at last, by the will of Almighty God, the Bait al-Kretliya was sold and passed from our ownership altogether.[3]

Now we Kretlis no longer have any part in the place, save that I still frequent and tend the tomb-chamber of Sidi Haroon as its guardian, even as my fathers did before me, the praise be to God.

As with the Bait al-Kretliya, so it is with the Mosque of Ibn Tulun. For let me inform you that long before our house had declined, this great building fell into disrepair and was abandoned, becoming the haunt of bandits and beggars, as well as of poor tradesmen. Among its great columns and spaces they made rope-walks and dyers' yards and placed tanners' vats and much else while, already, poor houses surrounded the mosque so that its

Translation of the inscriptions: "Here, in the year 565 Hegira, came the Sultan, the hero, the brave, the enlightened Salah ad-Din al-Ayyubi, and as he found that the Mosque of Ibn Tulun was empty and not in use, he turned it into a wikala in which to receive his foreign visitors." On the sleeve of the Sultan, left, "the pious Salah ad-Din." On the Koran which he reads, "In the name of God, the Compassionate, the Merciful."

walls could scarce be seen. Within its outer court hovels sprang up which were the abodes of gypsies, acrobats, singers, and such-like riff-raff;[4] there, too, was established a place for the poor (an almshouse), where were accommodated the indigent, both men and women.

But before these things had happened while yet the mosque, though no longer used as a place of prayer, was still a noble structure crowning the hill of Yashkur, Salah ad-Din al-Ayyubi (Saladin), seeing the building deserted and ruinous, had it converted into a *wikala,* a vast caravanserai for the reception of distinguished visitors, travellers, and ambassadors from all parts of the world who came to Egypt and were housed and maintained here as guests of the Sultan in all luxury, and without cost to themselves, for as long as they wished to stay: and it is said that the Sultan was wont to visit these excellent persons from time to time, here in the *wikala* into which the mosque had been converted, and to discuss with them topics which concerned the far countries from which they had come.[5]

At that time they would journey hither on shipboard across the salt seas to the mouths of the Nile and thence to this City, first by river and then by the Khalig canal, which passed close to the walls of the Mosque of Ibn Tulun, and this journey could be done without changing their ship, for in those days sea-going ships were so small that the canal would take them. It was therefore near the great Mosque that these strangers would first land, and thus arose the expression *'Lihad Tulun'* ('Up to Tulun') or *'Ala qalbaha li Tulun'* (literally 'On its heart to Tulun') which sayings are used to this day.[6] They arose through those persons who journeyed from abroad and knew not this country or its language, being advised to let no one persuade them, on any pretext, to leave their ship (as the evil-intentioned would like to have induced them to do) but to stay on board 'right up to Tulun.' Those expressions, were I to employ them now, would imply that nought could dissuade me from my set purpose.

Thanks be to Allah, of late years the great Mosque has been restored, its surroundings cleared, and it brought back once more to the service of God; and likewise in even more recent times, the Bait al-Kretliya has been restored by the Government and re-established and brought back again in all its beauty to habitation by your Excellency as Allah ordained: and may His blessing rest upon it and upon you always.

And now, my dear and honoured friend, I have related as you desired me all the Legends and histories that I can recall concerning the ancient House of my fathers, the Bait al-Kretliya, and its neighbourhood in which I have lived for over eighty years, Allah be praised, and may His blessing be upon this House and upon all those who enter it and upon you for ever.

'And now join me, my hearers, in blessing the Prophet, the Guide whose praise we should celebrate.' Oh God Bless Him.'

Notes

1. These reflections on the ruin and desertion of the Mosque of Ibn Tulun and incidentally, though at a much later date and in lesser degree, of the Bait al-Kretliya, reveal a wide divergence between the claims of hearsay and actual fact. Historically, after the fall of the Dynasty, when in A.D. 905 the last Tulunid troops were massacred and the wonderful faubourg of al-Qataii burnt and razed to the ground, only the mosque remained 'battered but unbowed.' Some few repairs were executed in the eleventh century but thereafter the place seems to have been used as an assembly-ground from which the caravan of the yearly Pilgrimage to Mecca set forth. In A.D.1296 its extensive restoration was undertaken by Sultan Lagin in fulfilment of a vow. After that there are records of its still being in use for its religious purposes, under Kait Bey, at the end of the fifteenth century, when it may again have been abandoned as a mosque. There is a strong local tradition that Saladin founded a caravanserai (*wikala*) for foreign visitors here but apparently no historical evidence exists to justify the claim. As for Sheikh Sulaiman's other statements, they obviously refer to very much later days and are probably more or less authentic.

   In 1856 Clot Bey, Mohammed Ali Pasha's medical administrator, transferred the unfortunate sick and insane inmates of the Muristan of Kalaoun to Ibn Tulun, which doubtless accounts for the mention of an almshouse in this Legend.

   During 1882 the Comité de Conservation des Monuments Arabes was inaugurated, and one of its original aims was to restore the Mosque of Ibn Tulun. This was, however, not undertaken until 1891, when the first modern and extensive clearance and reparation of the mosque and its enclosures were carried out. Since the 1914/18 war, a grant of £40,000, obtained through the good offices of Ziwar Pasha, then Prime Minister, has allowed of further expropriations and complete repair.

2. These gloomy speculations apply especially in the East where, by Koranic law, a property, on the death of its owner, is divided amongst his kin, inheritance being more or less automatically allotted according to degrees of relationship.

3. The Bait al-Kretliya was expropriated and acquired by the Comité de Conservation des Monuments Arabes on behalf of the Egyptian Government (Ministry of Education) in 1934 and, as I have stated in my Introduction, it was, at my suggestion, allotted to me for life under certain conditions in 1935. The Sheikh's outlook on that event was benignly fatalistic, for was it not the will of God that this should come to pass? His attitude towards me was, moreover, at no time hostile as might have been the case with one less kindly disposed than he: in fact it was always most friendly.

4. This 'dishonourable' period is mentioned in the Fifth Legend (see also its Note 6) and is dealt with visually in the lower half of the illustration to that Legend. There, the artist vividly depicts persons of disrepute fully described in Lane's Modern Egyptians. The vast acreage of Tulun's Mosque doubtless lent itself to the activities here mentioned. Much the same fate as attended Ibn Tulun's mosque overtook the mosques of Amr and al-Hakeem. Speaking of the former, Gabarty (18th century) tells of its being devoted to "musicians and ape-leaders, conjurors, mountebanks, and dancing-girls."

5. It is this period of Salah ad-Din's *wikala* (12th century A.D.) which is shown in the lower portion of the illustration to this —the great Saladin is seen seated with the open Koran is front of him.

6. From time to time one still hears the saying "*Lihad Tulun*" and "*Ala qalbaha li Tulun*" as expressions of determination, though neither is recorded in Burckhardt's "Arabic Proverbs." In spirit, the nearest English expression would perhaps be "I jolly well will..."

The Island at Aswan

The Island at Aswan

I had always wanted to possess an island at Aswan, and on it to build a little house for my habitation during December to February when Lower Egypt can be cold and uncomfortable. For over a year the governor of Aswan had been trying to procure such an island for me, and I had almost forgotten about it when a letter arrived in 1935 to say that he had succeeded in getting first refusal of Hassan Island, near the left bank of the Nile in front of the Cataract Hotel. It seemed suitable, so on a sweltering September evening I travelled to Aswan and the governor and I were rowed out to inspect it. I fell for it at once; soon the purchase was confirmed and it was mine.

In spite of my commitments with Bait al-Kretliya, which had just commenced, I was in such a fever of excitement over this romantic island venture that I set to at once and designed a little bungalow dwelling, with three of its rooms domed and a loggia running most of the way round. Scale plans were drawn and when they were ready I again visited my island. This time the Nile was low and what was my horror to learn that my neighbour had for the past few years been manipulating the flood currents of the river so that the channel between his and my islands was almost completely silted up. Great was my disappointment, but I soberly faced the fact that the Bait al-Kretliya would soon claim all my care and attention, so I decided then and there to re-sell my hardly acquired island to my neighbour, an acquisition for which of course he had doubtless been scheming. So that delightful plan never eventuated, and though one part of my wish had been fulfilled in that I actually possessed an island, that was but 'Dead Sea fruit,' since I never inhabited it and my 'magic casements' never opened on the Nile!

Translation of the inscriptions: "The two brothers Gayer-Anderson Bey travelled from Cairo to Aswan to build a house on their Island at the cataract of Aswan. 'Fadl Effendi' waited in Cairo. Drawn by the Artist Abd al-Aziz Abdu." On the canopy is the Gayer-Anderson crest (a tree and a lion holding a spear) and its motto "stand sure." Below this is "Gayer" and "Anderson" and by the figures of the twin brothers "R.G." and "T.G." Below the double-domed building on the left, "Aswan Island" and on the boat, "Going to Aswan."

The
End